Jaunts of the Mantis

By Jim Henderson

.

In writing this book, I must acknowledge the 40+ years of science fiction books, movies, TV shows, and tabletop, role-playing, and video games that fired my imagination. Thanks to Ben Weilert and Nanowrimo.org for introducing me to the challenge that led to me writing this book. Thanks to all those who encouraged me in this effort and thanks to my beta readers for plowing through and providing feedback. Most especially, thanks to my dear wife Rhonda for reading the book multiple times and for her valuable feedback, encouragement, and patience.

CONTENTS

PROLOGUE

Tixaya System: ... a moderately populated system near the edge of Republic space. The system is formed around a G V Yellow Dwarf star and contains eight primary planets, over 30 dwarf planets, and a sizable asteroid belt. Total system population is around 3.9 billion with most of that on the main inhabitable planet, Tixaya 2. There are also substantial populations on the larger of Tixaya 2's moons, on colonies on Tixaya 3, on the moons of Tixaya 5, and in several stations in the asteroid belt.

Tixaya 2 is located 0.9 AU from the sun, contains approximately 60% water, and has a diameter of 10,500 kilometers. It houses a major KSF base, a minor naval base, a marine battalion, and the primary office of the regional governor ...

Kremnaya Encyclopedia*

*All quotes from the Kremnaya Encyclopedia are taken from the 17th virtual edition published in 1211 I.E. by the Kremnaya Encyclopedia Publishing Co., Krax, with permission.

Kremniy Scout Force (KSF) Lieutenant Commander (LCDR) Ximon Sabo was a good-sized middle-aged man with thinning black hair. At 1.8 meters, 100 kilos, and spending almost half his adult life at low-gravity or zero gravity, he had long fought a valiant struggle against a thickening waistline and KSF fitness rules. Nevertheless, he'd had his uniform "let out" so it fit well for the occasion of his retirement. Well-groomed and in the black and gray uniform with the high-collared coat and numerous medals, he looked pretty sharp. He stood tall for his retirement ceremony, the recognition, nice words, and toasts by old acquaintances. It had all been very nice.

However, the event, and especially the preparation, had gotten somewhat tedious. Besides that, he was very anxious to be somewhere else, seeing something else.

During the retirement ceremony, he had been informed that he had been selected for the Auxiliary Reserve Command (ARC) and awarded the use of a surplus scout ship – the Kremniy Scout Ship Survey Craft (KSS SC)-1550-V." That "V" made it an old Vanguard class craft. The Vanguard class ships were between 30 and 40 years old, and the last ones had been withdrawn from service a year or two ago. He had hoped for any award but had really wanted a newer Explorer or Voyager class ship. Either would be eight to 15 years newer than what he got.

The KSF has a LOT of ships of various shapes, sizes, and age. However, the most common are the various survey craft. The Kremniy Republic never lets the KSF have as many personnel as it needs. Therefore, the KSF always has far more survey requests than it can handle and, more often than not, the limitation is personnel. A survey ship might last 40 to 60 years, but they only kept most people from four to 20 years. So, a few decades back, the KSF had started "deputizing" a portion of its retiring officers, appointing them to the ARC, and awarding them the use of a surplus ship. That "award" came, of course, with strings attached. While in the ARC, the recipient had to maintain the vessel, produce the ship for inspection every three to five years, and had to be willing to share "exploration data" from its travels with the KSF. Further, in case of a major war or other emergency, the ship was subject to recall to service with or without its captain.

The Kremniy Republic of Worlds (KRW) is a loose republic claiming approximately 250-star systems and a half trillion people. Its area can be described as a flattened sphere or a fat lens shape. Many of its 250-star systems are either thinly populated colonies or are completely unpopulated and undeveloped. Therefore, it has just under 100 member worlds with diverse populations, economies, and governmental systems. The KRW is a constitutional republic run by the Republic Senate, with a prime minister and an upper (Sage Court) and lower house (Congress). The capital is located on Krax, which it was relocated to 20 years ago in order to be nearer the geographic center of the growing Republic.

Humans make up the primary inhabitants of the KRW, but there are several intelligent alien species represented within the KRW or its neighbors. These include multiple variations on the general human layout, but with divergent genes, appearances, and optimal light, height, and temperature ranges; Canids - bipedal humanoids descended from canine stock; Cetas – semi-aquatic mammals created in ancient times by enhancing intelligence sea mammals; and others.

Portions of the KRW are former systems of the Interstellar Empire. When the Empire was rocked by civil war and severe economic and communications disruption, many star systems broke away. The losses in that civil war left the Empire seriously injured and too weak to try to re-assert control of former systems. What's left of the empire is sometimes referred to as the "Rump Empire" or "Remnants of Empire."

The KRW is bordered by remnants of the Empire, multiple small kingdoms and alliances of kingdoms, a variety of independent states, the Federation of Free Worlds, and an area of very sparse star systems known as "the Vast."

The Kremniy Scout Force (KSF) is a branch of the KRW military focused on exploration, mapping, and interstellar communications. It has a fleet of several thousand ships, though most are small and lightly armed. In active combat, its forces can act as auxiliaries to Kremniy Naval forces or (less commonly) vice-

versa.

The other big "catch" was that, if you were awarded a ship, your retirement pay was docked as compensation. The amount varied with how new and/or advanced the ship was. So, not everyone chose to enter the "ship lottery." If you did, you would "bid" on how new a ship you wanted, knowing that if you won, your retirement pay would dwindle. In Ximon's case, his ship would cost him about 25% of his retirement pay. If he'd gotten one of the newer ships, he might have lost 40 to 50%. After a decade or so, the ship would truly be his, but his pay would still remain at the lower lever.

Anyway, regardless of its age, he was anxious to see "his ship." So, he met the robocab he'd ordered and had it run him past the hotel he was staying at. There he changed quickly, hanging up his uniform coat for what he assumed was the last time. Then he caught another car to the KSF auxiliary shipyard, dock 34-B. On the way, he tried to picture what she'd look like.

When he got to 34-B, the dockmaster checked his ID and said, "Congrats, it's all yours. It should be keyed for you," and let him in. As he entered, the dockmaster advised, "Remember, you have to have her out of here within 30 days."

There, sitting in a dusty bay, was KSS SC-1550-V – a ship clearly past its prime and in questionable repair. She appeared structurally sound, but he guessed it hadn't flown in a month at least. Her paint was faded with a remnant of some nose art, and her hull pockmarked. He instantly loved her but was somewhat cautious in his affection – like getting to know a woman who looked good, but you wondered what kind of baggage she had.

He tapped his tablet to the scan pad by the main ramp and waited. After a few seconds or so, the light turned a faint green and the port opened. He walked every inch of her.

Though there were several different versions or classes,

all survey craft were small, cheap, flexible vessels used for all manners of exploration and scouting missions. Most could jump nine to 12 light years through "folded space," had pretty good acceleration in normal space, could mount a small weapons turret, some defensive weapons, and virtually any reasonable kind of sensor or experiments. The hull was also aerodynamic so it could enter most planetary atmospheres. Their engines were very robust, and the ships were all equipped with skimming scoops that could suck up gases in the outer atmosphere of most gas giants to use as fuel.

The Vanguard class was designed under the theory that a slightly larger survey craft would be capable of some missions that previous versions weren't. Thus, they were approximately 30% larger than most earlier survey craft, displacing just over 130 tons. The concept didn't prove to be that useful or cost effective in most cases, so subsequent classes slimmed back down to an average displacement closer to 100 tons.

KSS SC-1550-V had one of the more common interior layouts with a three-seat bridge, six cabins, a common shower room, a decent sized galley/common room, and multiple optional sensor ports. She presently had no turret, no defensive weapons, and only had a basic sensor array.

She was clearly old but seemed in decent shape. The capacitors held a stable charge, the computer was online and responded to voice commands, and the systems only showed a few warnings in a trial pre-flight check. All survey craft had moderately advanced artificial intelligence built in that can handle basic functions, provide a degree of autopilot, monitor alarms, do some basic planetary scans and medical diagnostics, etc. It's a necessity when sometimes a single scout is operating light years from any assistance. Hers seemed pretty good, though somewhat outdated.

He picked out what he thought would be his room, did various system checks, and started making a list of the supplies and fixes she'd need. He took a lot of images, keyed the ship to his comm link, customized a few settings, and headed home to plan next steps.

As was so often the case with retired scouts, he had the ship, but no real plan. So, he needed to work on that while getting the ship checked out mechanically. That meant he needed to hire a mechanic, at least to inspect her, and possibly to sign on for a while. Luckily, KSF maintained a ready list of recently retired scouts who were willing to entertain work. So, he planned to start contacting some in the morning.

He slept soundly and contentedly, dreaming of past service and potential space adventures.

When Ximon awoke, he considered rolling over to sleep a lot more since this was his first day of "freedom" after having been in the KSF for two-and-a-half decades. However, after laying there a few minutes, he decided he was too anxious to get working on his ship to go back to sleep. He pulled up Scout-Link – the KSF's platform for scouts, and former scouts, to stay in touch. He needed a mechanic, and this was his first place to look.

Ximon spent a while perusing profiles of ex-scout mechanics who said they were available for short-term or long-term work. He focused on people with extensive maintenance experience, including relatively recent experience on Vanguard-class craft. Partway through his searches, he had to expand his definition of "relatively recent." The last Vanguards had been retired about a year ago and little maintenance had been done on them since then. Eventually, he had 10 or 12 reasonable candidates and sent messages to his top five candidates. He asked about their Vanguard experience and their immediate availability for work of some duration. Then, on second thought, he sent similar messages to the next three or four. Then, he had to wait.

He spent some time daydreaming about ship names.

Since they had so many, the KSF didn't name most survey craft other than their designation, such as KSS SC-1550-V. That was their official name in the records. However, most ship captains named their ship something if they were assigned for more than a few months. That nose art remnant probably represented some recent captain's name for her, but Ximon couldn't make it out in the images. Since he and the ship were in the ARC, he couldn't formally change her name in legal records or on its transponder. However, he could call her whatever he wanted, and it had to be good.

He carefully studied the images he had taken the day before and started making a list of some supplies he knew he'd need to "take her out." He soon decided he needed to go survey the ship more to make a better list. So, he got up, got breakfast, made himself presentable, and headed to the dock.

Ximon spent several hours surveying the ship, checking supply cabinets, tool racks, etc. In general, the supplies were pretty sad. He'd have a lot to buy, though he could do some of that over time. While looking, he received several short responses to his job messages. A couple weren't actually available, one was in the hospital, a few more weren't available for a month or so, etc. However, as the afternoon dragged on, he did get positive messages from two potential candidates. Both had attractive backgrounds, including some relatively recent Vanguard experience, and both were available ASAP.

He had brief video interviews with both, made sure their experience sounded legit, that they didn't seem like jerks or slugs, and got their reactions to maintaining a Vanguard. In all, the two seemed pretty comparable. He reviewed their profiles in more detail and reached out to some old friends to see if they knew of either, but both were still pretty even.

Ultimately, he called Elsbeth Petra on a virtual coin toss. Well, he considered it a coin toss. However, it did cross his mind that, if he ultimately signed her onboard, he'd rather share a ship with a decently attractive 40-ish woman than another guy in his 40s or 50s. He'd been on enough long trips in enclosed spaces to see some guys get REAL CASUAL, and he had no desire to see them walking around in their underwear. He was also a practical guy and he knew that many men (himself sometimes included) could be pigs and that was less likely with a woman.

"Elsbeth, this is Ximon Sabo, would you be able to do a thorough inspection on that Vanguard in the next few days?"

This had been notionally discussed in the interview, so she was quick to reply, "Should be able to, but it depends on what you mean by thorough, on whether I can bring in a few other guys, and on the pay. If you pay me enough to bring in a couple guys, we can do a pretty good inspection in about two days. That's nowhere near as comprehensive as a depot inspection, but it'll tell you what you need to know. I can go deeper if you want, but it'll take more time, manpower, and money."

Ximon wasn't at all surprised at those stipulations. "Sounds fair. Could we meet and set things up tomorrow?"

"Sure, I can come by mid-day and exchange documents. I'll start lining up a couple guys, assuming that all works. Let's see – it's Tuesday, so I'll try to have them ready to start Thursday."

That sounded good to him. "Ok, let's plan to meet around 1200 tomorrow at the ship. It's dock 34-B."

"Wouldn't make sense to meet anywhere else. I'll be there and I'll want to poke around a bit."

"Roger. I'll have the docs ready. See you then."

She arrived just before 1200 the next day. He greeted her and led her up the ramp to the small galley where he had a few images and a few beers and sodas ready. He noted that, Elsbeth was, indeed, moderately attractive, curvy with long sandy blond hair. That never hurts, especially when you might be flying with someone for weeks or months. Her record showed she was in the KSF about 20 years, had served on a variety of ships and spent some time on stations.

Ximon showed her a few images of the ship, explained what he wanted in the inspection, and proposed an amount.

She seemed unphased. "I'd like to walk around a bit. Give me 20 minutes." Then she grabbed a beer and her tablet and started walking.

After about 30 minutes, they met back. She had taken some images of her own and some notes.

She led in, "She's not going to win any races or beauty contests, but at a glance, she seems like a decent ship. However, you've got no supplies or tools to speak of. It's worse than many of these ARC babies. I'll need 800 cr more than you proposed to buy or rent a few things. If that's acceptable, I can start tomorrow around 9:00. I'll have one guy then and another coming a little later."

Republic Money and Measurement:

Money: ... within the Republic the primary unit of currency is the credit. This is typically abbreviated as cr and is typically shown after the number. Larger amounts are typically shown as thousands of credits (Kcr), millions of credits (Mcr), or even billions of credits (Bcr).

Measurement: The Republic uses the standard measurement system inherited from the Interstellar Empire. This system is based on an archaic measurement system known as the metric system that supposedly flourished on a semi-mythological "origin world."

Time: Similarly, the Republic measures time using an anciently derived system featuring seconds, hours, days, months, and years of a standard length. No one is quite sure why the lengths are what they are ...

He could see how his savings could vanish fast if he

wasn't careful. "OK. Give me just a minute to make the mods and I'll send you the docs for certification."

They shook on that and it was a deal.

Elsbeth arrived with a young technician named Jake and a cart full of supplies and toolboxes just before 0900 the next day and got right to work. Ximon tried to stay out of their way but couldn't help but peek occasionally and had to act as another set of hands on a few things until another technician, Ivan, arrived that afternoon. As far as he could see, they seemed to be very thorough and pretty efficient. One guy was an older retired scout, the other a young technician with diverse experience, but no scout time. At one point, he even took off to go get some items to stock his room and the galley. With Elsbeth's team working, he should have thought of the galley earlier, so he made sure they had plenty of snacks and drink additives.

The next morning Elsbeth and team arrived around the same time to work. By mid-morning, she told Ximon that she'd be done by around 1800 that night and she'd present her report to him the next morning. She was good to her word, and a little later, she told him they'd be packing up shortly and she'd like to present her findings around 1030 tomorrow. The technicians wouldn't be back, so he thanked them profusely when they left and kept their contact info.

The next morning, Elsbeth set up for a presentation in the galley like she owned the place. She sent him a document report, but her presentation was largely visual. She started out, "Ximon, here's what we found," and launched into a 45-minute visual presentation with lots of explanatory graphs showing variances from ideal. She kept a beer in hand or nearby.

There was both good and bad news in the report. She hit some of the highlights as she ticked them off on her hand and displayed data graphs:

"The jump drive appears sound, but the magnetic array

needs a serious adjustment. You could easily mis-jump if you used it as is. The maneuver drive looks OK, but several maneuvering thrusters are broken. The fuel system needs a major cleaning and all filters replaced. It looks like she was running on skimmed fuel a lot and her filters weren't doing a good job. The computer seems stable, but it and the nav system need a million updates. The communications array needs alignment, or you won't be able to talk more than 100K or so."

She paused, took a drink, took a breath, and continued. "Scanners need alignment too or fidelity and range are both dubious. The reactor could use some alignment, but its output is good and no leaks. Artificial gravity, never good in these models, needs some parts to get above 20% standard. The main airlock and ramp are fine, but port airlock is broken and can't be used, starboard airlock inner door needs repair. Cargo doors are good, but the lift is shaky and slow."

Again, another drink and another breath. "The air raft is a classic, and not in the good sense. I certainly wouldn't attempt re-entry in that and probably wouldn't want to fly very high. It'll cruise through town, but that's about it. We didn't do a full run down of minor stuff -- electrical, plumbing, lights and fixtures, but I noted quite a few that need fixed. So she needs some work to be considered "sound," but there are only a few things that MUST be fixed before you take her off planet and a few more before you try to jump with her. The good news is that, though a lot of things need repaired, aligned, or tuned, I noted few major components that actually needed to be replaced. So, she won't be an immediate money pit."

Ximon was a bit dazed at the length of the list but was glad that he didn't need to buy a new reactor or anything huge like that.

All he could say was, "Well, I knew she didn't just come off the assembly line, but it's sobering to hear the list."

Elsbeth looked askance at that. "I assumed you were paying me to find the reality."

"Definitely, and I can't blame you for that reality. It is what it is. So how would you recommend fixing this?"

"Well, the fastest and easiest thing would probably be to turn it over to a ship depot facility. They'll go over it in detail, fix everything major, and give you back a nice, pretty ship."

He started to interrupt, but she went on, "However, I'm sure you don't want to spend that kind of money. So, you have two options."

She put up two fingers and pointed to the first. "One, you can hire a mechanic team to fix everything before you fly. That'll probably take about two weeks."

Then, she pointed to the second. "Or you can hire a mechanic to fix the key stuff, then fly her easy with a mechanic on board, and they can fix a lot of things while in flight."

He figured those would be the options. "How would those compare price-wise?"

"Well, in the first, you'd pay me or some other mechanic team to fix a prioritized list of things. That'd probably be a contract at cost, plus a certain amount per day. In the second, you hire some mechanic as crew for a while, they fix what they can before you fly, and then fix what they can while you fly."

"That's about what I thought. I'm looking at some jobs on ScoutLink and I'd like to take one that's about six to eight weeks long. If you're open to a short-term contract, I'd like to hire you as soon as you can start. If not, I'd like to hire you to do some of the most critical repairs while looking for someone else. What do you say?"

She looked pensive and thought for a minute before saying, "I'm open to that if you can get the tools and supplies I need, and we can agree on a price. I could probably start on Monday or Tuesday. Would the crew just be you and me for this trip?"

"I think so for this one, but I do have a humaniform bot, Raiza, that does a little light work and can be an extra set of hands if you need them."

Elsbeth snorted and smirked at that. "Sure, humaniform and helpful – an extra set of hands whenever you need them, eh?" Then she chuckled to herself and said, "Never mind, no surprise to me and none of my business. Certainly not the first one I've worked around. If your bot can do some useful work and you don't mind her getting her hands dirty, she could help."

Ximon could tell that Elsbeth was assuming that Raiza was a sex bot. Raiza could and did serve that function at times, but Raiza DID do some other useful work. Raiza was a TrueForm Service Robot (TSR) model D8 companion bot. She was about 1.6 m tall with a small waist, a relatively large bust, a dazzlingly beautiful face with some permanent makeup, and strawberry blond hair that fell in ringlets when not in a perfect braid.

Elsbeth's amusement reflected a common joke that all scout ships, or scouts, had sex bots. While not technically true, many ships, or scouts, did. Some scout missions had crews of one to six scouts away from port for weeks or months, and it could get it awful lonely. It was not uncommon for some members of scout crews to "hook up" or even get married. The KSF never broke down and bought bot "assistants" for their ships, but most ships were equipped with awesome virtual reality (for analyzing scan results and planning missions) that was often used for porn. In any case, scout crews, as well as long-range transport crews, were prime "target markets" for the makers of sex bots. Many individuals or crews would buy or rent one when they could. But Ximon, of course, bought Raiza to do work around the ship to save him time. It just so happened that she looked, felt, acted, and moved like a woman. His logic, such as it was, was that human-like bots worked best in human spaces and ships.

Elsbeth went on, "So let's talk price and supplies ..."

Then they dove into negotiations. Neither side was too set on a specific "deal," so they soon reached an agreement. Elsbeth provided Ximon with an initial list of supplies to order and Ximon said he'd send the contract the next day.

Over the next couple days, Ximon set himself (or the ship) up as a company, got a finalized contract with Elsbeth, took out a small business loan, ordered the supplies and tools that Elsbeth dictated, and generally stocked the ship. He (and Raiza) also officially moved into the ship and set up Elsbeth with access codes so she could come and go once she started work.

Then, he requested an appropriate basic scan mission off the ARC job board. The KSF always had requests or tasks that it couldn't fulfill, so it would farm some of the basic ones out to its ARC personnel and ships. These didn't pay a lot, but it was enough for some repairs and to keep the ship flying. It was also work that the ship was well suited for and which Ximon (and Elsbeth) was accustomed to. So it was good job for a test trip. Ximon got the job and set an estimated start date about a week out, which Elsbeth said should work.

Elsbeth did start on Monday and got right to work. Ximon helped when he could or when asked, and Raiza did prove useful, fetching and carrying, serving up tools like a surgical nurse, and helping position large, bulky objects. When Ximon wasn't helping Elsbeth with repairs, he did detailed planning for the job, plotting their likely route, jump points, etc. Elsbeth gave him daily updates on repairs and frequently ordered more parts and such. The ship was, indeed, going to be ready as planned, so he informed the ARC job office of their departure plan for the next morning and they agreed to meet at the ship at 0700.

The mission was to take updated scans of the Avar 4, the fourth planet of the Avarian system, and its moons. The KSF would issue them two upgraded sensors and some small cubesats for the mission. The Avar system has been surveyed before and there was a small mining station on asteroids sharing an orbit with the fourth planet. However, long range sensors suggested some strange atmospheric activity on Avar over the last few months. The last official survey of Avar4 was over 10 years ago and anecdotal data from passing ships was sparse and unremarkable. The star Avar was located 15.3 lightyears from Ximon's home system of Tixaya and the ship had a jump range of 10.6 LY. Thus, they'd need to first Jump to an intermediary system, refuel, and then jump to Avar. Ximon planned to jump to the Taupra system, which has a few small colonies and two stable gas giants that can be skimmed for fuel.

> *Jump: Interstellar travel is primarily accomplished using the hyperspace jump drive. The jump drive creates an intense gravo-magnetic field arrayed in such a way that it allows the ship to enter an area of folded space that allows much shorter travel to its target destination. Safely jumping requires extremely detailed navigational projections accounting for all sizable gravitational fields. It cannot safely be performed within several astronomic units (AU) of a standard star, nor too close to a planetary body. If the navigational planning is poor, there are major gravitational anomalies near the destination, or the jump drive malfunctions, a mis-jump can occur. In a mis-jump, space is not folded properly to allow travel to the destination. In minor cases, this can lead to the ship coming out of jump many thousands of kilometers from its target point, but in severe cases, it could lead to the ship crashing into a planetary or solar body or being transported to a star system located light years (LY) from the destination. The number of LY that a ship can jump at one time is known as its jump range, jump capability, or jump speed. Jump ranges are typically between 5-25 LY.*

When Elsbeth arrived, Raiza had a good breakfast waiting and Ximon had a quick announcement. He picked up some juice and said, "In honor of this trip and this grand venture, I've come up with an official name for this ship. Though her transponder may say, 'KSS SC-1550-V,' she shall be called Mantis! It may be all she has, but hopefully she'll give us that. A toast to Mantis."

Elsbeth didn't appear overly impressed, but pursed her lips, shrugged, raised her glass. "Mantis," and drank her juice down. Raiza did the same with her juice, though she had no need of food or drink.

Ximon continued, "OK, with that out of the way, let's get this baby in the sky. Elsbeth, take a few minutes to finish your food and get settled. Then let me know when you're ready to monitor things in Engineering while I pre-flight and take off."

He then directed his voice at the air generally. "KSS SC-1550-V, you are now designated as Mantis. You will respond to voice commands by that name as well as KSS SC-1550-V. Confirm."

Mantis's smooth female voice responded, "Designation Mantis confirmed, Captain."

Mantis:

Type:　　　*Survey Craft*
Displacement: 130 tons
Power Plant:　Closed Fusion Reactor
Thrust Rating: 3.1G
Jump Range:　10.6 LY
Sensors:　　*Basic KSF planetary / ship package*
Computer:　*Type II Basic Ship Control*
Armament:　None
Defensive Systems: None
Crew:　　　*1-8 officers and enlisted personnel*

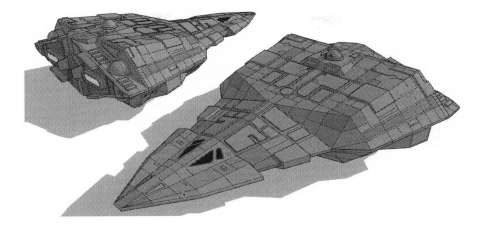

JAUNT 1: A MEETING AT AVAR

Elsbeth scarfed down a few more quick bites of breakfast, said, "done," and headed to her room with her duffel and backpack. She was a practiced hand on a ship, so she came on comms from engineering within about 10 minutes saying, "All readings look good so far."

Ximon finished pre-flight checks, got clearance from the control center, and eased Mantis up. She handled fairly well under easy acceleration and they were soon headed for the edge of space. Once they'd finished their main acceleration, Elsbeth joined him on the bridge since she could monitor almost everything from there. They both watched carefully while enjoying the flight until they got out of the gravity well of the planet. Ximon said, "Our first stop will be the Taupra gas giant where we'll top off by skimming. ETA 19 hours to jump point to Taupra."

Elsbeth nodded. "Understood. I'll need to watch the purification levels carefully when we do that to ensure we don't 'gunk up the works' again. She seems to be running well. I'll keep monitoring while working on some of the many remaining issues."

Ximon said, "Roger. Let me know if you need me. I'm putting her on auto-pilot and will do some more planning for our destination."

He then added, "Mantis, monitor all systems for operating within tolerances and direct any anomalies to my tablet as well as ship consoles. Alarm on any safety-critical systems until directed otherwise."

"Yes, captain. Monitoring all systems and alerting as directed."

Ximon checked and rechecked his jump calculations and studied the available data on both the Taupra and Avar systems. The flight to a safe jump distance was uneventful, or almost so.

Ximon was zoning and almost dozing, monitoring progress when the ship klaxons sounded, shocking him out of both his reverie and his seat.

Mantis said in an authoritative tone, "Captain, ship water pressure is operating 10% outside of safe tolerances! Prompt corrective action should be taken!"

Elsbeth immediately chimed in on the circuit, "What the hell's going on up there?"

Ximon said, "Hold on, Elsbeth," then went on, "Mantis, did I not direct you to just send alerts for anomalies?"

The ship replied, "Captain, you directed me to immediately alert you of any safety-critical system operating outside safe tolerances. The water system is safety critical in that it is vital for both the sustainment of biologic organisms, but also because it is involved in the operation of fine maneuvering thrusters and in the cooling of key system components."

Ximon groaned. "Elsbeth, you get all that?"

"Of course, and I know the water pressure isn't at standard levels. I told you that. It's fine and I've got it shunted so we have more than enough pressure in the systems and areas we're using. Just turn off the dang alarms or it's going to be a really long trip because we've still got a lot of things outside tolerance."

"Roger. Mantis, just send alerts of anomalies. Do not alarm on anything except imminent collision, fire, or explosion."

"As you say, captain. However, I should quote from the KSF Ship's Operation Manual 127-4 'The maintenance of survey craft is vital to the mission. Virtually any ship system can become safety-critical if not maintained properly.' Therefore, I must suggest that this be repaired as soon as practical."

Ximon and Elsbeth angrily responded almost in unison, "Noted. Now shut up!"

They made it out to Ximon's calculated jump point with no further incident. Though Mantis advised of multiple system anomalies, neither Elsbeth nor Ximon noted anything of immediate significance. The selected jump point was well beyond the system's main gas giant and selected so that the next planet was at the farthest point on its orbit (i.e. on the other side of the sun). Thus, they were outside all of the largest gravitational fields.

Ximon signaled Elsbeth. "Elsbeth, we're at the jump point. I'd like to jump in 15 minutes if you're not in the middle of anything that would be affected."

"Well, I'm in the middle of something, but it's not related. I'll just make sure stuff's not going to fly around and will let you know as soon as I'm ready. I've put in extra monitoring checks and should be able to see any deviations or distortions. Though once the jump has started, it'll pretty much be too late."

Ximon groaned again. "Great, and thanks for that. Let me know. The main ship's view will be on image channel 7 if you care to watch."

He strapped in, double checked all the key settings, and waited to hear back from Elsbeth.

As soon as he did, he counted down, "Initiating jump sequence in 10, 9, 8 ...." and then pushed the button to initiate.

Initiating a jump wasn't actually all that dramatic. There was no huge acceleration or deceleration and usually no turbulence to speak of. However, momentum did sometimes shift, and you did tend to feel a lurch in your stomach and inner ear. Some described it like a fast deceleration in an elevator or the first exposure to zero-G and it did nauseate some people. So, it was customary for all personnel to at least be seated and not have a lot of loose gear around when it was initiated.

Like many, Ximon liked to watch the stars as the jump began, but some found that view disconcerting and avoided it religiously. There wasn't a whole lot to see. You'd be starting at a huge number of stars, then the stars would appear to move as if you were dizzy, and then....NOTHING. When the ship jumped, the engines created an intense gravo-magnetic field that put it in any area of folded space that allows much shorter travel to its target destination. It would generally take four to seven days to "traverse" this space and come out at your destination. However, within this space everything just appeared to be a black void and there was no sense of motion and nary a star to be seen. Again, some found this earth-shattering, but it just told serious spacers that it was time to get back to other work or get some rest. Elsbeth did the former while Ximon did the latter.

Over the next six days, Elsbeth made a lot of progress fixing systems both minor and major with a lot of assistance from Ximon and Raiza. Ximon and Elsbeth chatted a lot as they did so. Ximon knew that Elsbeth had retired after 20 years, but he hadn't known that she had been married once and in a civil union another time. She had no kids, but she was close to a couple of her sisters and their kids who all lived on Tixaya. She was (or considered herself to be) the "cool aunt" that had adventures and brought back fun souvenirs and pictures. Ximon was familiar with that role. He too had a few siblings, nephews, and nieces that he occasionally saw and stayed in touch with.

Elsbeth appeared to wear the same old pair of scout coveralls most of the time, though she could have several near identical sets. On day four, she said she was "taking some time off," and he only saw her meandering around in flannel pajamas and bare feet as she raided the galley for food and drink. One time when he saw her, she appeared to be a bit tipsy. That would have been alarming during regular flight, but in mid-jump, there was little that could go wrong and, if it did, there was nothing you could do about it.

On day six, Mantis signaled all, "We will be leaving jump in the Taupra system in eight hours. Prepare for return to inertial space and ensure you are fit for duty if on duty." This was a traditional reminder to ship crews to stop drinking if they were, wake or get to sleep as appropriate, and prepare for what could sometimes be a bumpy ride. She then repeated this at four hours, two hours, one hour, and then 10 minutes form jump termination.

As the time counted down, Ximon chimed in, "Leaving jump in 10 minutes. Strap in and monitor for issues."

He didn't have to do anything to exit jump – it was all pre-calculated. However, he did have to be ready. As the ship left jump, there was always a lurch (sometimes small, sometimes huge), and then a sudden return of inertia as you typically left jump at roughly the same velocity you had when you entered it. Therefore, you didn't typically want to be pulling serious Gs when you entered jump because it would hit you hard when you came out and went from zero to several Gs all at once.

Ximon had stopped their acceleration before entering jump, so they came out with speed, but no acceleration. There was a sizable lurch, but that wasn't too concerning. His first task now was to verify their location and that everything was OK.

"Mantis, get me a fix – three stars then five. Elsbeth, how's everything looking?"

She responded immediately. "I'm still reviewing the monitors I put in. It looked pretty good, but the field still needs some tuning. I'll let you know if I see anything else."

Ximon checked all the area sensors for any unexpected objects but found nothing of note.

Mantis responded long before he finished. "Captain, we are in the Taupra system, exiting jump within 5,000 kilometers of the planned exit point."

Ximon did some more active scans for debris, ships, etc., and found nothing noteworthy.

Mantis noted, "Five-star fix confirmed. Taupra system, exit at 1,278 kilometers from nominal."

That wasn't great but wasn't bad. They made it in one piece and hadn't hit anything. The ship still had some life in her.

Ximon got ready for the next steps. "Mantis, adjust course to the Taupra 5 gas giant for deviation from nominal and notify when ready. "

Then he quickly scanned for signals. There were no signals aimed at them, but he found a standard message from the Taupra 3 mining colony and put it on speaker. This message could act as a beacon of sorts as well as a welcome message. It also periodically announced upcoming issues and events. It announced a few upcoming competitions and several outages, as well as a few reminders to conserve water and practice good environmental suit discipline for safety.

Mantis soon notified Ximon that she had optimized and checked the course to Taupra 5 so Ximon set course there and announced, "En route to Taupra 5 for skimming operations. ETA 14 hours. Elsbeth, please check skimming and filtration systems." He then started a series of standard long-range scans and just watched the stars for a few minutes before leaving it in Mantis' hands and heading to his room for a quick nap.

As they approached Taupra 5 later that day, Ximon checked atmospheric density and composition scans against library data. There was no discrepancy, so he adjusted course to skim the out atmosphere and announced, "Skimming will commence in 15 minutes. Be prepared for possible turbulence. Elsbeth, I'm lowering the scoop."

Skimming: ... most interstellar spacecraft operate, or can operate, off hydrogen. Being one of the most common elements in the universe, it isn't hard to find. However, finding it in enough density to be worth gathering was less common ... unless one went to a gas giant. Most gas giants contain enough hydrogen or other useful elements in their atmosphere, and at enough density, to make it worthwhile. In skimming, a vessel equipped with a scoop cuts through the outer atmosphere, gathering up the gases there. It then vents the useless ones and sends the useful gases, primarily hydrogen, through the filtration system to top off the fuel tanks. It is the cheapest way to get gas and works well as long as the ship has a good filtration system and cleans that system pretty regularly. Skimming can also save time, by allowing ships to avoid the need to negotiate with a space station to buy fuel. The skimming operation usually takes between 30 and 60 minutes, depending on atmospheric density and the size of the ship's fuel tanks and scoop system ...

Ximon guided Mantis through the outer atmosphere and started skimming. "Elsbeth, please watch the filtration system for purity."

"Roger. I'll let you know if we're not getting good stuff out the other end."

They did this for just under an hour before Mantis announced, "Fuel tanks at 100%."

Ximon announced, "We're full. Retracting scoop and initiating 1G acceleration to next jump point. ETA 11 hours."

Other than sharing a few messages with a freighter inbound to the Taupra 3 mining colony, the run out to a safe jump point was uneventful as was the jump initiation.

While in jump for the next five days, Elsbeth led them in fixing a lot of minor things. She also sent Ximon a running list of some of the additional parts and supplies he'd need to purchase when they got back home. It was minor stuff but there was a lot of it.

Other than that, they just got to know each other better. They had a few mutual old scout friends, had similar tastes in music, and were seemingly more comfortable leaving home and coming back than in just BEING at home. Elsbeth attributed the breakup of her marriage to this tendency. Ximon could relate – he'd never been married, but several relationships had failed, in part, due to this.

Ximon also doublechecked his mission plan and checked out the additional sensors and the small cubesats that he was issued for the mission. They all checked out OK, so they should be good to go when they got to Avar.

They came out of jump at Avar without incident. Ximon confirmed that they were in no immediate danger. Mantis quickly confirmed they were out past Avar 7, about 220 kilometers from nominal insertion point.

Ximon checked in, "Elsbeth, status?"

"Everything's looking good. No anomalous readings and the jump field is getting better tuned."

He didn't immediately detect any communication activity from the Avar 7 station, but sent them a greeting signal, "Avar 7, this is the KSS Mantis inbound for a survey at Avar 4. Please advise of any known navigational or other concerns." It would take about 30 minutes round trip to get a signal back from them, so he just filed that away.

Then he announced, "Initiating 1G burn to Avar 4 in 10 minutes. ETA 17 hours."

G burn: ... Even in vacuum and zero gravity (zero G), accelerating or decelerating with maneuvering engines imposes acceleration forces on a ship and its passengers. Within the Republic this is represented as percentages of the forces of gravity (G) as calculated on some ancient 'origin' planet. Many ships produce

no artificial gravity and these acceleration Gs are the only time
they're not in zero G. Many other ships can produce a degree
of artificial gravity, though the percentage of 'standard' 1G they
can produce and sustain varies. In any case, the Gs caused by
acceleration still apply, producing forces on space travelers ...

As soon as the course was laid in, he started doing scans of the general vicinity and long-range scans of Avar4. He directed Mantis to alert him if Avar 4 data deviated dramatically from historical data. Then, except for a quick break for lunch, he watched intently as they headed in.

In about an hour, Ximon got a video message from the Avar 7 station. A tired-looking middle age man in gray coveralls sat in front of a faded seal for the station. "Greetings Mantis. This is the Sven Thompson at Calton Mining Station at Avar 7. There are no imminent navigational concerns. However, the last freighter in, Atomist, which arrived two days ago, did note two distant ship contacts that didn't respond to hails. We checked with the other mining sites and it wasn't any of theirs. It could have been a sensor ghost or something but thought you should know. If you're interested, we'll send you some scan data from our area. Let me know if that data is of use to you and, please, let us know if you see anything we should be aware of. We don't have any operations near Avar 4, but have ships going past to some inner stations."

Ximon responded, "Roger Calton Station. Thanks for the insight. We would appreciate any data you have. Please send by compressed burst. We'll let you know if we see anything of note. Good luck and good mining."

Elsbeth joined him as they were about an hour out from Avar 4, "Thought I'd see how the other half lives." She grinned, "Actually, I thought you could use a hand with the sensors, and I wanted to understand the plan for deploying those cubesats. You'll recall we didn't repair one of the airlocks. So, tell me more about your latest plan."

"Well, we'll focus our scans on Avar 4 as we approach, but we'll be able to get some shots and scans of the second moon on the way in. My plan is to do about a day of varying orbits of Avar 4, possibly more depending on what we see. In the process we'll deploy the cubesats for max coverage. They'll keep gathering data and will relay to us as we're leaving and then will send periodic data to one of the stations to send to the next comm boat that comes through."

"Sounds reasonable, but what's the plan for deploying those cubesats?"

"Ah, my thought was to have Raiza in a suit in the cargo bay basically toss them out. Once out, we'd do diagnostics and then fire thrusters to get them in a stable orbit. Am I missing something?"

"Well, that could work, but two things: One, there is a cargo manipulation arm in the cargo bay – I could use that to deploy them if you want. Two, if you want someone to sling them out the cargo bay, I could do that – I might have a better arm than Raiza. Oh, and three, does Raiza really need a suit?"

"If that arm is working, then I guess that'd make sense, though I'd want someone in the bay in case there's an issue." Then he continued somewhat sheepishly, "The manufacturer recommends that Raiza not be exposed to vacuum or the cold of space – it reduces battery life and can make her skin brittle."

Elsbeth grinned like an idiot and was almost unintelligible with laughter, "Well, of course, we simply MUST keep Raiza full of energy and soft AND pliable, eh? Wink, wink, nudge, nudge." With the last, she nudged him in the ribs and then really broke down in laughter.

Ximon tried to look serious, but had trouble suppressing his own laughter. "I'll have you know that Raiza is a valued member of this crew and as Captain, I have a solemn responsibility to protect the wellbeing of my crew. And she's been of some help to you. You never know, she might save your life someday."

She continued to guffaw. "Oh, of course, great Captain. Solemn responsibility…must ensure she stays," she chortled. At this, she leered, "FULLY functional." Then she continued, "I'll run some diagnostics on that cargo arm. Am I right that second moon will come up to Starboard as we go in? I'll do the scans on that as we go on and can run one of the other sensors as we get closer to the planet." Then she laughed to herself again, "I think they're fully functional too. Perhaps you might want them for some company, eh?"

Ximon simply had to say something. "Well, I'm certainly glad I could provide you with some humor. Part of my solemn duty to my crew, I guess."

"Oh, and you make it look so effortless."

"It's a talent."

Mantis chimed in, "Captain, you directed me to alert you if scans deviated from historical data. It appears that atmospheric readings have deviated across at least four chemical components, some higher, some lower. You'll see the list on your screens."

He read them off. "Oxygen, Nitrogen, Argon, Carbon. Hmm, and that's not a small difference. Thanks, Mantis, we'll check all those with active scans. Continue scanning for any debris or gravitational anomalies. Elsbeth, that moon will be coming up on the starboard in five minutes. I'll be entering orbit in about 15 minutes."

"Roger," responded Mantis. "I'll get as many images as I can and do a basic battery of scans."

They entered orbit without incident, scanning continually on multiple scanners. Ximon had Mantis hold the orbit so he could focus on the atmospheric scanners. The readings were definitely very different for numerous elements. He couldn't think of anything that could account for so big a difference from the historical data unless the historical data was corrupted somehow.

"Elsbeth, please conduct a detailed magnetic mapping and compare to the data."

"Roger, I think I can do that with Mantis' help."

Ximon hit the comm link, "Raiza, please bring up two sandwiches and some water bottles."

As they got about halfway through a 90-minute orbit, Mantis alerted, "Captain, I'm detecting an object in orbit. Its size appears consistent with an unidentified (UI) artificial satellite, but it's approximately 3,000 kilometers toward the South Pole from us. We'll need a closer pass to determine its composition and purpose. I recommend that a subsequent orbital pass get closer to its path."

"Roger, I'll tend South for our next orbit, but we won't be too close for a couple orbits."

After about 30 minutes, Elsbeth chimed in. "Ximon, I finished that magnetic analysis. It's different too. The field is stronger than recorded and it appears more stable. I can't see anything to account for it."

Ximon responded, "What the hell is going on here? Well, I guess that's why we're here."

Avar 4:

> *Diameter: 14,200 km*
> *Surface Water: 50%*
> *Distance from sun: 1.2 AU*
> *Atmosphere: Moderate density. Moderately caustic with low oxygen content (Historic). Low-grade caustic with moderate oxygen content (Revised).*
> *Gravity: 1.1 G*
> *Temperature Range: -10 to 50 C*
> *Magnetic Field: Low and erratic (Historic). Moderate and mildly erratic (Revised).*
> *Lifeforms: None detected*

As they swung around, Ximon directed, "Mantis, get all the images you can of that UI satellite you noted. Elsbeth, please check out that cargo arm. I want to deploy the first cubesat in about an hour."

Then they continued circling. As they did, Mantis noted, "Captain, the images of the UI satellite are indeed consistent with a satellite monitoring the planet." Then, a couple minutes later, "Captain, the UI satellite is periodically transmitting bursts of data toward the outer solar system. I'm collecting what data I can and will analyze."

"Good call. I'd like to know what it's saying."

"Elsbeth, how's that arm?"

"It looks fine, Ximon. I'm going to have it pick up Cube 1."

"Roger. Raiza, suit up and assist Elsbeth with Cube 1."

"Yes, Captain."

"OK, Elsbeth, once you're sure it's ready and Raiza is tethered, position her where you need her. I want to deploy that in about 25 minutes."

"Got it. We'll be ready. I'll make sure your precious crew-mate is safe and where I need her. Then I'll come up and control the arm from there."

When she left, he signaled Raiza, "Raiza, make sure you're properly tethered and stay back unless we direct you to engage. Be careful."

Her response was far less formal than normal and almost a whisper. "Of course, Ximon."

Elsbeth returned in about 20 minutes and took the sensor operator's position, "The arm, the satellite, and the robot are all ready. I'll open the cargo door and deploy the arm on your mark. It'll take three to four minutes."

"OK. Then go ahead and start. Get that baby out there."

"Rog. Opening cargo door now..."

As Elsbeth deployed the arm, Ximon pinged Mantis. "Anything more on that UI sat?"

"Negative, Captain. I will inform you when I have any more details on the UI satellite or the data."

He also pinged Raiza. "Raiza, how's it looking down there?"

"Captain, the arm is extending properly with the cubesat. Everything is stable in the cargo bay."

Elsbeth spoke up, "OK, Ximon. The cubesat is away. It will auto-orient itself, but it'll need a thrust vector to get into a stable orbit."

"Roger. Already on it. Mantis, send the vector coordinates I laid out to Cubesat 1."

"Yes, captain. Command stream sent to Cubesat 1."

They carefully monitored the cubesat as it got into a stable orbit. This one was orbiting about halfway between equator and South Pole in the general vicinity of the UI satellite.

"Ok, Mantis, we'll be coming around for a relatively close fly-by of the UI sat in about eight minutes. Try to get all the data you can. Oh, and Raiza, go ahead and take off the tether and suit if you hadn't already. It'll be several hours before we need to try that again."

"Already done, Captain. I'm testing and stowing the vacc suit now."

Elsbeth looked at him with mild chagrin. "Do you really think I left it just standing there in the cargo bay? That would kind of seem ... jerk-ish. I may not have a personal robot, but that doesn't mean I'll go out of my way to cause them grief. And, by the way, her suit would have run out of power if I just left her there."

"Ok, thanks. No one had said anything."

As they continued orbiting, they came within several hundred kilometers of the UI sat. Mantis scanned it and took images. Mantis compared data and put some images up on the main viewscreen.

Elsbeth noted, "The specific layout doesn't appear common, but it's clearly some kind of observation sat. It looks like it has some kind of cameras and, perhaps, some spectral analysis equipment. It's clearly monitoring something on this part of the planet. Also, as Mantis noted, it's sending a burst of data, apparently near the same point on each orbit. The data appears compressed and probably encrypted. No clue what it is so far, but it's a good bet it's similar to the atmospheric and mapping data we're gathering and what we just put that Cubesat out to do. So, we don't know who put it here, how long it's been here or who it's talking to, but there are a lot of possibilities. It could be a mining corporation considering some new exploration, someone doing a scientific study, or ...."

Ximon, "Or possibly something alien ...."

Elsbeth demurred, "Yes, possibly, but so far there's nothing to suggest that's most likely."

"Perhaps. Mantis, keep trying to crack the data and see if you can triangulate where those signals are going. We're going to do one more orbit and then go stationary above the South Pole for about an hour. When we're there, I'd like you to rerun those magnetic field scans. That'll be in about an hour."

"OK, I'll try to be back up, but I've got to do some checks on that arm – it worked but seemed shaky." She got up. "You know, it's just possible that we need another crew member, perhaps one whose expertise is scanning, science, and stuff."

Ximon smiled. "Flexibility is the key to the KSF, Elsbeth, you know that."

"Sure … or it's a sign of bad planning." She said as she ducked out of the bridge.

"Yeah, yeah … there's always that."

The remaining orbits to the South Pole went without incident and Elsbeth did additional magnetic field mapping. "Ximon, it shows the same kind of changes as the previous data – a stronger, more stable magnetic field. No sign what might cause that, but if we had an actual science officer…"

"Yeah, thanks. Ok, we've been at this a while. Elsbeth, why don't you get some rest. I'll catch a nap while Mantis winds us back up toward the equator. We'll take about five hours and then deploy another Cubesat there." He then directed Mantis to take a spiral course up toward the equator, collecting imagery and sampling as they went. He also had Raiza come to bridge to monitor as "another set of eyes" and went to his room for a nap and a shower – he was feeling pretty ripe.

Ximon came back in about four hours and Mantis and Raiza were both observing intently.

Mantis informed him, "Captain, we have completed four

equidistant orbits. If we continue this trend, the next one should approximate the equator. I have not deciphered the data from the UI satellite, but it appears to be numeric in nature. The transmissions appear to be targeted at a region encompassing a 15-degree arc from this planet, 10-20 degrees of the orbital plane of this planet, to an area 28-30 AU from the sun. "

Raiza also reported, "Ximon, you look well. I'm glad you got a good rest. It's comforting to have you back at the helm. While you were gone, I noted no alarming activity nor anomalous behavior."

"Uh, yeah."

Then he signaled Elsbeth who showed as working in engineering. "Elsbeth, I'd like to deploy Cubesat 2 in approximately 50 minutes."

"Roger, I was just about to head that way. Raiza, please join me in the cargo bay."

A short time later, they had made another orbit and deployed Cubesat 2. It seemed to go OK and they were able to get the Cubesat into a stable orbit. However, Elsbeth noted, "Ximon, that cargo arm is having issues. I'm not a 100% sure it'll work for the next one, but I'll try to work with it before we get up to the Northerly orbit that I assume you have planned for Cubesat 3."

"Right, you've got about three hours before we deploy it. Let me know what you find."

They orbited a few more times, collecting more data, more images, etc. Ximon gave a 30 minute to deploy warning and Elsbeth and Raiza went to set up.

When it came time to deploy, Elsbeth again operated the arm from the bridge. However, it soon became clear that something was wrong. Specifically, it became clear when Elsbeth said, "Dammit. What the F---------- G—D--- B-------? What kind of moron maintained this thing?"

The arm had gotten stuck just a couple meters outside the bay and could not release the cubesat.

Elsbeth said, "It appears the hydraulic lines have broken. I can't get any motion other than a shimmy out of it. I can try to fix it, but I think that'd take four to six hours. If you want to deploy it now, I worked out a plan with Raiza."

"Roger. Raiza execute the plan as directed. Exercise extreme caution."

"Yes, Captain."

Ximon heard Elsbeth directing Raiza, "OK, as we discussed, move along the arm being careful not to tangle your tether." Then after a short pause, she said, "OK, grab the two manipulation points on the Cubesat and I'll release the arm's hold."

Ximon was alarmed to see Raiza sitting on the arm like a bicycle and grasping the satellite.

Elsbeth continued directly calmly, "OK, the arm has loosened contact. Rotate 60 degrees and execute the simultaneous push maneuver with your arms as we discussed."

Ximon could then see Raiza basically shoving the cubesat into open space. That worked well, but the inertia spun her off the arm and out into space as well.

Ximon yelled, "Raiza!"

Meanwhile Elsbeth coolly continued, "OK, Raiza, orient yourself to hold your tether in two hands. Ok, now start pulling, I'm going to reel your tether in."

Ximon could see Raiza swinging about somewhat around the cargo door of the ship and hit the opening a few times, but she was soon inside. Ximon was running for the cargo bay before Elsbeth closed the door.

By the time Ximon got there the internal airlock to the cargo bay was just cycling, so he was able to go in. Raiza lay on the deck attempting to disentangle herself. Ximon rushed to help her and Elsbeth came up behind to assist. They soon got Raiza untangled and upright.

Ximon said, "Raiza, what's your status?"

"I am fully functional, Captain. However, I'm detecting several alarms on the suit."

Ximon and Elsbeth both helped her off with vacuum suit but noted issues as they did.

Ximon noted the alarms and suit condition anxiously. "The faceplate is cracked and there's a tear in the suit. If she was human, she might be dead."

Elsbeth tried to calm him. "Yes, but those would be at best minor leaks. We'd likely have gotten her back in time."

"Maybe, but it shows we need to be more careful."

Elsbeth replied with some heat and somewhat defensively, "Sure, and that we need to get more stuff fixed."

Ximon directed Raiza to do a complete diagnostic in his quarters. Elsbeth rolled her eyes and said, "Heading back to engineering."

Ximon continued orbiting toward the North and just had Mantis check the magnetic fields there. The results were similar, though not as different from historic data as in the South.

Ximon declared, "OK, everyone, we've finished the primary survey of the planet. Get some rest and some food. We'll head to the moon in seven hours." He then directed Mantis, "Maintain station-keeping orbit here. Continue scans. Alert me of any other ships or debris."

He went to his quarters, did a much more detailed inspection of Raiza for damage, and got some sleep. He awoke rested and Raiza already had some breakfast and coffee ready for him. She brought it to him on a tray. "Good morning, Ximon."

"Well, breakfast in bed. What a surprise."

"Since I was here, I was able to monitor your breathing and predict when you'd likely wake. From there I made the breakfast items you most commonly eat. I also washed some of your clothes and have laid out a fresh uniform for you."

Ximon had to admit that was pretty nice. He didn't always have Raiza spend the night in his quarters, but there were obviously benefits (other than the obvious) to doing so.

"Thank you Raiza. Are you feeling well?"

"Yes, Ximon. I do not believe I suffered any damage from yesterday's satellite deployment, and I always feel better after sleeping with you. It brings me great pleasure and I enjoy being able to care for you."

"Well, Raiza, that's a great quality in a woman or anyone. I'm comforted by your presence as well."

Ximon spoke to the ceiling. "Mantis, is there anything to report?"

"Nothing to note, Captain. Ship functions are all normal and I have detected no other ships or satellites. I have continued analysis of the UI Sat data. Making some assumptions, it appears to be numeric data related to atmospheric conditions."

"Thank you, Mantis. I'll be up in about 30 minutes." Then, he noticed that Raiza was still there, undressed, and fully functional. "Correction, I'll be up in an hour. Please block comm requests unless it's an emergency."

Ximon left Raiza cleaning his quarters and headed up to the bridge happy and well rested. Once there, he did a quick scan of instruments and glanced at the latest scan data – nothing earth-shattering.

"Good morning everyone. Everything appears nominal. We'll conduct a 1G burn to orbit the first moon in 20 minutes."

"Elsbeth, how's everything in engineering?"

He didn't get an answer, so repeated that.

An exasperated Elsbeth came on the line. "I'm not in engineering. I'm taking a frickin' shower. I was up late fighting with that arm. I'll be up to the bridge in 20 minutes so we can discuss the plan." Then she added snarkily, "I guess we all had fun with machines last night," and cut off.

Elsbeth came up about 15 minutes later. She too appeared well rested and less haggard than normal. She brought her breakfast with her and sat down in the science officer spot and turned toward him. Then she said, "So tell me the plan," and took a big bite of some kind of muffin.

Ximon explained to her (and via speaker) to Mantis and Raiza, "We'll burn toward Moon 1 here in a few minutes. We'll do about eight fast mapping/scanning orbits there. If we don't see anything, we'll then burn toward Moon 2 and do the same.'"

Elsbeth swallowed and motioned vaguely to the screens. "Shall we talk about the elephants in the room? We've got a UI sat that pops up to monitor the planet we've been set to monitor and it's beaming data to what appears to be a dead zone at the edge of the system." Then she took a few more bites.

Ximon continued, "I was getting to that. Assuming we see nothing on those moons, we'll do a slingshot orbit of the planet and our planned jump point will be near that area of space. Keep in mind that it may just appear to be sending data there. For all we know it could be some survey satellite from some of the miners that's got its antenna pointing the wrong way."

Elsbeth chimed in, "Oh, sure. That's the most likely thing," as she gulped coffee.

"I didn't say it was the most likely thing, but it IS possible. If there are no other questions, prepare for burn in 5 minutes."

Elsbeth smirked and made a mock salute, "Aye, aye, Captain Crunch."

The orbits of the first moon were uneventful. They took various readings, and nothing appeared any different from historical data.

The second moon was a different story. On their first pass, Elsbeth chimed in, "Ximon, I've got a structure on the surface of the moon facing the planet. Mantis, keep scanning that, enlarge the images and put on screen."

They then stared intently at it. It appeared to be a small building though its purpose was unclear.

Ximon touched his screen to mark the spot on his digital maps. "I'll bring her right over that spot and lower and slower on the next pass."

Since the second moon was small, that was only about 10 minutes. They again scanned eagerly and took lots of images. The structure appeared to be only about 5 X 15-meters square, with what appeared to be antennae or instruments sticking out.

Ximon said, "I'm thinking it's an observation post. Mantis, do you detect any signals?"

"Captain, it has a faint power signature. It's not transmitting, but a source 150 kilometers away is transmitting bursts of data."

"What the heck? Let's go check that out."

He veered Mantis over there and circled as they scanned. This just looked like an antenna field.

Mantis added some additional highlights to the map on the screen. "Captain, the signals appear similar in form and direction to those from the UI satellite."

Elsbeth said, "Well, SOMEONE is sure interested in our little planet here and they appear to be out there in dead space."

Ximon nodded slowly. "Yeah. We'll stay in orbit here while I transmit the initial report. I'll plot a course out there.

Elsbeth, make sure we're ready to maneuver."

She nodded and left the bridge muttering to herself. "Uh, yeah. If we had any weapons, I'd go check all those, but no such luck."

Ximon spent the next hour finalizing an initial situation report (SITREP) on Avar 4 and its moons, noting the changes in atmosphere and magnetic field, the UI sat, the UI structures on the moon, and the signal destination. He then transmitted it two ways. First, he sent it to the comm relay on the mining station. Whenever any other scout ship entered the area, it would retrieve those stored messages. Second, he sent out a comm buoy. This essentially a tiny probe/satellite that would simply wait for any scout ship to relay messages to. The cubesats would also send periodic updates to both the mining station and the comm buoy.

Elsbeth came on radio. "Did you just send out a comm buoy? Ok, I can see where your heads at." She knew he was a little concerned.

Ximon came on radio. "We'll be doing a half-G burn toward a jump point near that comm target area in 10 minutes."

"No hurry, I see. I quite agree."

"ETA to jump point 17 hours. Everyone, listen for direction to strap in, we might need to maneuver fast."

They left orbit and headed toward a jump point within 50 kilometers of the comm target area. Raiza joined him on the bridge and sat her arm on his shoulder. "Ximon, can I be of any assistance or do anything for you?"

A few thoughts came to mind, but he just said, "Yes, thank you. Please, sit with me and help me watch for anything anomalous."

She sat down in the co-pilot chair. "Certainly, Ximon. Please let me know if there's anything else I can do."

"Your presence helps."

They moved along for a few hours, when Mantis intoned, "Captain, I'm detecting what appears to be a vessel at long range. I will track it to judge range, vector, and velocity but it will take 10 to 20 minutes due to the distance lag. I will take some long-range images as soon as possible."

"Roger. Raiza, please refill my water bottle with mild stim and bring both me and Elsbeth a sandwich."

"Of course, Ximon."

He then radioed Elsbeth. "Elsbeth, if you're not tied up with anything down there, please join me on the bridge. We have a contact."

"On my way." She appeared almost instantly and plopped down in the co-pilot seat, staring intently at the viewscreen.

As they continued to approach, Mantis provided an update, "Captain, the vessel appears to be on a direct contact vector at approximately 0.6G. Mass is estimated at 1,000 tons. Here are the first images."

Ximon and Elsbeth stared at a small, blurry image.

"Well, Ximon, that tells us nothing. It looks generally obolid and it's not smooth, but we could be looking at a battleship, a trash hauler, or the universe's biggest torpedo."

Ximon tapped some spots on the screen. "Mantis, focus on that for chemical analysis and keep trying to get better images."

Raiza brought them food and drinks, and then strapped into the sensor operator seat.

Ximon then sent out a message to the mining station, "Calton Station, this is Mantis, we've completed our survey and will soon be leaving the system. We're investigating a vessel at our planned jump point, but no data so far."

Ximon said, "I'm going to try hailing them."

He directed a message at the approaching vessel. "Approaching vessel this is Kremniy Survey Craft Mantis on a routine survey of the Avar system. Please identify yourself."

They were hit by loud bursts of data on virtually every open channel. It came across as a loud squelch on the open channel.

Mantis noted, "The signal is similar to the data previously detected, but more varied."

"Roger, Mantis, try to make some sense out of it."

As they continued to approach, Ximon repeated the message every 15 minutes. The ship seemed to respond shortly thereafter each time. The data was unintelligible but seemed to be changing.

After about 90 minutes, Mantis displayed some better images. It appeared to be a fairly normal asteroid but seemed to have a few structures on it.

Elsbeth stared at the screen intently. "My readings are in sync with what we're seeing. Its composition appears to be primarily dense rock, but with some man-made superstructure."

Ximon repeated the message. This time the response definitely appeared to be a mix of garbled words with the data.

Ximon smiled. "It's getting clearer."

They continued approaching, continued scanning, and continued sending the message. The response got continually clearer.

Finally, they could understand at least some of it, "Kremniy Survey Craft Mantis //garble// Greetings this is //garble//. We ask your intent on our //garble//."

Elsbeth noted, "Well that was almost helpful. Ximon,

let's send them more data."

"Huh?"

"They might be trying to understand our language."

"Ah, yeah. Mantis, please send them the traditional first contact welcome from the Republic. That's about 1,000 words and should give them something to chew on."

After a few minutes Ximon repeated his message and added, "We are on a peaceful survey mission. We intend no harm to your vessel or your operations. What is your intent?"

Several minutes later the vessel responded, "Kremniy Survey Craft Mantis thankful for kind greeting. Greetings this is //garble// vessel 4 of the People. We value your peace. Why have you surveyed a planet that we have claimed for our use?"

Ximon groaned and announced to the crew, "Oh, brother. Looks like we may have a resource dispute."

He sent the other ship another message. "People of Vessel 4, greetings. We have surveyed this planet because our leaders claimed this system and this planet long ago. Our leaders directed us to survey it because it appears to be changing and they wish to know why. We were unaware of your presence or your claim."

The other ship responded as quickly as lag would allow. "Kremniy Survey Craft Mantis, this is planetoid vessel 4 of the People. Your people could not claim this planet as they have done nothing with it. Therefore, we have claimed it for the People and are fixing it."

"People of Vessel 4, are the changes we have seen on the planet a result of your fixing?"

"Of course, Kremniy Survey Craft Mantis. We are modifying the planet for our use. We have travelled far and need a home to bear many young."

"We understand and are impressed with the speed of

your modifications. We will notify our leaders and they will wish to discuss the use of this planet with you. They may be able to assist."

"Kremniy Survey Craft Mantis. We will welcome any assistance. Advise your leaders of our ownership of this planet."

"People of Vessel 4, we will advise them and encourage assistance. You said you have travelled far. May we ask where you have travelled from?"

"Short name Mantis, we travelled from our home system as our sun became unstable. We have been travelling for 213 orbits of the home of the People around the People's sun. Please view this diagram of our home."

They then sent an odd but readable star system diagram. It showed numerous star systems with unreadable notations but seemed to indicate they came from approximately 17-star systems away.

Onboard ship Ximon whistled at what the diagram suggested. "Holy crap, they've travelled 17-star systems in something like 213 years. They're clearly travelling sub light the whole way. They must have a generation ship or a sleeper ship."

Then, to the ship. "Vessel 4, we thank you for the insight. You have, indeed travelled far and your need of a home is understood. Do you travel solely with thrust like that you're using now?"

"Mantis, yes. It is the most efficient means available to us. We can reach velocities of approximately 67% of the speed of photons in a vacuum when not affected by external gravitational effects. We observed your vessel arrive in this system but did not see how. Do you use other means to travel?"

"Vessel 4, yes sometimes we use something called hyperspatial jump travel. We are few on this ship and of limited understanding. But when our leaders discuss assistance, they may be able to explain this to you."

"Mantis, that would be of great assistance. Please tell your leaders of our desire for assistance and hyperspatial jump travel."

"Vessel 4, our leaders will be able to offer better assistance if they understand your People better. May we ask how many of the People are with you?"

"Mantis, the people are many, though far fewer than on our home world. On Vessel 4, there are 30 of the People. In our other vessels, there are several thousand and thousands of eggs."

Elsbeth chimed in internally at that. "There are thousands of them, and they lay eggs. Ximon, I think it's about time to get out of here."

Ximon shushed her with a hand gesture. "Maybe, but I've got just a few more questions."

Ximon had Mantis send Vessel 4 an encyclopedic entry about humanity and about the Republic.

He then contacted them. "Vessel 4, we have sent you some additional information about our people and our leaders. The information includes some pictures of them. Please, let us know if you can access this information and the images."

"Mantis, we have received the information and thank you for this gesture of peace. However, it will take us some time to understand it. We can see the images, though your people appear strange indeed."

"Many alien races appear strange to one another until they establish peaceful relationships. Could you send us an image of your race so that our leaders may better establish peaceful relations with you?"

"Mantis, we value peaceful relations. Please receive this image of our people as a gift of peace from the People."

Elsbeth let out a yelp when the image appeared on the main screen. "What the hell?"

The image contained several dozen individuals on a planetary surface with a strangely colored landscape and sky. At first glance, the People looked a fair amount like a more upright combination of an ant and a praying mantis. The People pictured varied considerably in size, presumably including young. However, there was no definitively sized object to compare to.

Ximon said internal to Mantis, "Interesting. They appear insectoid. I wonder if they evolved from some insect or evolved separately in a separate way."

He then contacted the Vessel. "We appreciate the opportunity to understand your people better. As discussed, we will report back to our leaders that they may offer assistance and establish peaceful relationships. To do this, we will continue on this course for approximately 25% of the distance from the planet to the sun. We wish you peace, success in your modifications to the planet, and many young."

"Mantis, we welcome peace and encourage you to leave this system as you propose. We will continue to the planet, but another of our vessels will meet you soon to escort you to the point you name."

On internal comms, Elsbeth said, "They apparently don't want us strolling through their other ships. But Ximon, you'd better say something about the cubesats and about the mining colonies."

"I was trying to find a time to work that in. I guess that's now."

"Vessel 4, we will welcome the escort of another vessel of the People. Two other things I must mention as we part. First, we have deployed several artificial satellites around the planet that we may understand it and, thereby, better understand you. "

"Mantis, why would you seek to learn about a planet we

have clearly claimed?"

"We were not aware that you claimed it, so our leaders asked us to learn more about it. When our leaders discuss things with you, this knowledge will help them offer assistance."

"Mantis, understood. We will not obstruct these artificial satellites if they do not harm us."

"Thank you for understanding. The other thing I must mention is that there are other humans working on other planets and asteroids of this system. We will ensure they do not bother the planet you claim, but we must ask that you don't disturb them or the ships visiting them. They have claimed these other planets and asteroids and our leaders would not understand if you interfered with them."

"Mantis, we have noted the other humans at range, but have not contacted them. We will respect their claims if they respect ours. They must not visit our planet or interfere with our ships."

"Certainly. We will inform them to not interfere or visit."

"Mantis, very well. Please tell them that our leaders would not well understand if they did."

"Vessel 4, of course. We all value peaceful relationships."

"Mantis, as do we. We must continue to the planet. We look forward to meeting you again in peace."

"Vessel 4, as do we. Thank you."

They all breathed a sigh of relief after that exchange.

Elsbeth said, "I'm going to have nightmares about that one. Those things were creepy, like giant bugs."

Raiza looked at her quizzically. "Per my observation, they appeared insectoid, not arachnid. As you know, insectoids are the most common complex life forms in Republic space."

"Yeah, whatever. They're still creepy."

Ximon interrupted their exchange. "In any case, we've got a few things to do before we jump. First, I've got to issue a Notice to Spacecraft. Second, we've got to talk to that guy's buddy when he contacts us. Third, I've got to send an addendum to our report. Elsbeth, could you take the conn and talk to that other vessel? Alert me if anything appears to be 'headed South.' I'm going to go to my room to write this crap up. I'll be back in about 60."

Elsbeth took his chair. "Sure. I'll try not to start an interstellar war."

Mantis noted every so helpfully, "An interstellar war would be most unwelcome ..."

Elsbeth cut her off, "Yeah got it. You just like them because they look like your namesake. What the hell are the odds of that?"

Mantis responded, "I'm not entirely sure what namesake you're referring to. However, the odds of two species that evolved separately appearing similar are fairly low."

Ximon went to his cabin and pounded the keys. In about 20 minutes he had a draft notice that he asked Mantis and Raiza to both proof for accuracy and consistency. They both agreed that it properly reflected the situation accurately. Ximon then had Mantis send it to all the mining stations and send it to be forwarded to travel advisories. It read:

NOTICE TO SPACECRAFT

System Affected Avar (837B-7V).Issue Date 348149 101937

Issued by: Kremniy Survey Craft 1550-V, the Mantis

By order of the Kremniy Republic of Worlds, no Republic of allied vessel is to approach within 100,000 kilometers of the planet Avar 4 or interfere with any alien vessels transiting there. The KSF has initiated first contact protocol with an alien race that is conducting peaceful operations there and at the following Avar system coordinates ... Any violation of this order is punishable by ship confiscation, loss of license, or imprisonment. Republic representatives will return to conduct follow-on negotiations. Please forward any questions to the nearest KSF Office or the regional governor.

About that time, Mantis was hailed by another vessel.

Elsbeth answered, trying to sound officious in a tone like Ximon, "This is Kremniy Survey Craft Mantis. We welcome you in peace."

"Kremniy Survey Craft Mantis, prepare to receive and send video as a sign of peace."

Elsbeth adjusted her hair unconsciously and sat up straight then accepted the video.

An image appeared that looked to her like a giant praying mantis sitting in a chair and playing with controls. A few smaller figures were visible in the background scurrying about (in her mind) like cockroaches. It made her skin crawl.

"Short name Mantis, this is Planetoid Vessel 11 of the People. We are to accompany you to a point for approximately 729 //garble// to a point agreed upon with Vessel 4 of the People. We greet you in peace and will leave video communications open that we may better understand you in peace."

Elsbeth suppressed a cringe and tried to stay focused on her controls. "Greetings Planetoid Vessel 11 of the People. We will travel to the agreed upon point at our current velocity and will not deviate from this course."

"Understood Mantis. Your people are, indeed, as strange as //unintelligible clicking// 4-74 indicated, but we welcome peace."

"Vessel 11, in understanding there is peace."

They then travelled on in silence, having nothing in particular to say. Elsbeth felt like it was sizing her up for dinner and tried to avoid eye contact.

A short while later, Ximon finished his addendum to their survey report and had Mantis forward it to the mining station and the comm buoy. Then he returned to the bridge. Elsbeth happily gave up her seat, tried to move out of view of the screen, and studiously avoided looking at the screen.

"Mantis, this is Planetoid Vessel 11 of the People. I am confused. You creatures appear quite distinct. Which one of you is the creature that //unintelligible clicking// 4-74 communicated with?"

Ximon, now in his seat, said, "Vessel 11, I am the one he communicated with. I am known as Ximon and I lead this ship. May I have your name?"

"Mantis, very well. There is peace in understanding. My name is //unintelligible clicking// 11-27. I lead this vessel of the People."

He signaled Mantis to play back that name then added, "... it is an honor to converse with you and see you."

"Mantis, yes. We value peace."

They then flew on in silence until they approached the point. Mantis detected at least eight vessels of varying sizes near the comm target point. Ximon had her take extensive images.

Ximon had everyone prepare for jump and asked Raiza to prepare dinner for after they jumped.

Vessel 11 spoke up. "Mantis, our data indicates that you will reach the agreed upon point in 18 //garble//. We ask that you depart as agreed that we may all enjoy peace."

"Vessel 11, we depart in peace as discussed. We will leave now ..." and he pushed the button to engage. The stars waivered, they all felt a lurch and they disappeared from the Avar system to the nothingness of jump.

Elsbeth tore off her headset. "That was some weird crap. I'm going to take a quick shower before dinner. All jump readings look nominal."

Ximon followed not long after. He noted Raiza was still making dinner and thanked her. She said, "You're welcome. Dinner will be ready in 15 minutes. Then, if you have no other tasks, I'll go do a complete diagnostic."

Ximon nodded and headed to his room for a quick shower and a new jump suit.

When he got back, Raiza was just setting dinner and drinks out. Elsbeth arrived a few minutes later, carrying a bottle of wine. She looked quite nice. Her hair was loose of the braid she typically wore, and she had quite a mane. And he'd swore she was wearing makeup and perfume.

Ximon pointed to the table. "I think we've got some here."

"Sure, but I wanted to get a head start." The bottle was clearly open and down a glass or two.

Ximon motioned to the table. "Well, dinner's ready. Have a seat and let's eat. You clean up pretty well."

Raiza sat down the last few items and poured them the wine she had selected. Then she left.

Elsbeth started cutting her food. "That was a bizarre encounter. Those things made my skin crawl. I'm not sure if I'll sleep for a week."

"They weren't that bad and first contact is always exciting."

"I think if you look at the history, first contact often goes poorly with some death and destruction pretty common. We got lucky they were reasonable bugs, but I don't know what the Republic is going to do with them. Those bugs will be pissed if the Republic shows up and tells them to leave."

"I don't think it'll come to that. If the People are willing to be a protectorate or something, the Republic will let them stay as long as they behave themselves. We obviously have some technology they can use, but I think we might have some things to learn from them. That terraforming they were doing looked pretty dramatic in a short period of time. I'm going to emphasize that in my formal report. I think it might work out if the People and the miners avoid each other."

"Maybe, but if someone goes back and all the mines are slag heaps full of half-eaten bodies, I wouldn't be surprised."

"So melodramatic."

"So you say, but I'm telling you it looked like that guy was sizing me up for dinner and I don't want no bug chewing on me. Like I said, I'm betting on nightmares."

Then they talked about some of the things they still had to do as they travelled back. Ximon needed to finish his more complete, formal report on the trip and prepare mission invoices. Elsbeth had a few more minor repairs she wanted to work on and then she had to finish her list of supplies and parts that the ship needed. She warned Ximon that it would be sizable.

Ximon shook his head in some frustration. "Well, I'm new at this accounting. I'll turn in the final report when I get there and file the invoice. They supposedly pay fast and then I'll get you your share and buy those parts. What are your plans for after this? Are you up for another contract?"

"I'm open to that if you can get those parts, I can hire a mechanic to help for about a week when we're back in port, and you try to find another crewmember. We were AWFULLY short-handed there."

"True, but it worked out, right?"

"Only by luck. You know that we could have used some-one who could have better understood all that scan data. That COULD have been essential to dealing with those things, but luckily, it wasn't."

"Just yanking your chain. I plan to try to find someone, but I've got to get the pay first. Would you consider a 6-month contract?"

"I'm up for that IF we can meet those conditions. Oh, and I'd like the new crew member to be a super-hot, desperate boy toy."

"Not at the top of my list, but you never know."

They kept eating, chatting, and drinking until all the food and the handy wine was gone. Ximon was a tad fuzzy, but he thought Elsbeth might be more so.

Finally, he said, "I've got to crash. Looks like you could use some rest too. Catch you in the morning."

"Sure, leave the girl to clean things up."

"You don't have to get it. Raiza will."

"Still a girl. I'm arguing for solidarity."

He shook his head and headed for his room. "G'night."

He got ready for bed, but then worked on his report for a bit before turning in. He was afraid he might forget a few things if he slept on it.

About 45 minutes later, there was a knock on his door.

He opened it and there was Elsbeth in pajama pants and a sports bra. He'd never seen her without coveralls on and she REALLY filled out that bra.

He stared as he tried to think of something to say. "Uh ...."

"Ximon, I wasn't kidding about those things giving me nightmares. I've tried, but I can't sleep. Can I sleep with you tonight?"

"Uh, that's not a good idea."

"Why not? What's wrong with crewmates bunking together? I know you've done it before."

"Yeah, but it's often a bad idea."

"Look. We're mature adults. I'm scared and I'm lonely. You might be lonely if not for Raiza. But give a real girl a chance.

"You're drunk."

"Just a little and I've made far worse decisions sober. Look, let me sleep with you even if you can't stomach anything else. Please."

"Oh, it's not that, and it has been a long while since I've been with a real girl. Come on in and we can see where it goes."

"Great. We can always pretend it never happened if we want."

Ximon knew from experience that was rarely ever possible, but he was interested enough to overlook that reality temporarily.

Ximon woke up to the sound of gentle snoring next to him and paused to admire the body. He concluded that, yes, this had probably been a terrible idea, but Elsbeth was an energetic and vocal companion, and it was nice to wake up next to a soft, warm, real body. *Oh well*, he concluded, *not much we can do about it now. We'll just have to see what kind of crazy it brings.* Then he got up quietly, went to take a shower, and got dressed.

Elsbeth woke up when he came back to the room. She looked confused at first, then far more embarrassed by her naked body than she'd been last night. "OK, I'm going to steal this blanket and leave. Forget I was ever here." Then she scuttled out of the room, holding the blanket around her.

Ximon went about his day waiting for the crazy to hit – accusations, blame, etc., but it never did. He didn't see Elsbeth all day, but she got Raiza's help a couple of times for some repairs she was attempting. Ximon kept working on his report and sent Elsbeth the "Ship's function and mission support ability" to fill out – her responsibility as engineer.

The rest of the jump was uneventful. The report was finished, some repairs made, and generally quiet trip. Likewise, coming out of jump at Taupra, refueling, and going back into jump toward Tixaya was uneventful.

As Ximon and Elsbeth ate a large lunch that day, Ximon asked her, "Are you still game for a six-month contract? If so, I'll get those papers to you."

"Why the heck wouldn't I be? Sure, get me the papers, but I'll wait to sign until I get paid, if that's OK with you."

The trip was pretty quiet for a couple days. Then one night he heard a knock on his door. It was Elsbeth, "I'm having nightmares again. Can I sleep with you?"

He just motioned her in, and they had a fun, but restful night.

She snuck out in the morning while he was in the shower and never said anything else about it.

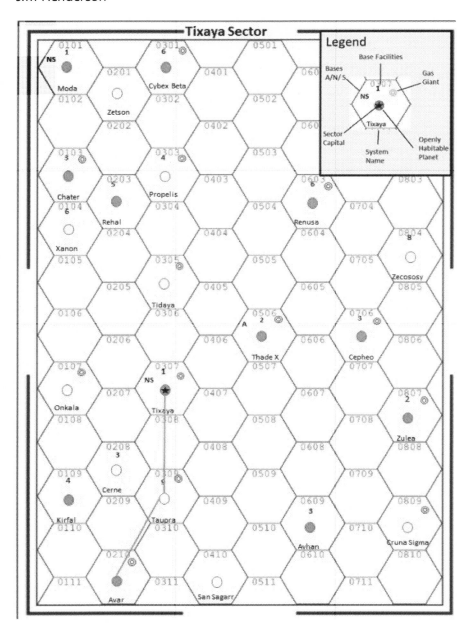

They came out of jump out on the far side of the orbit from Tixaya 5. Then they headed in to Tixaya 2.

"Prepare for a 1G burn to Tixaya 2. ETA 16 hours."

Once they got moving, Ximon transmitted his final report to the KSF base, directed Mantis to monitor the trip, and just spaced out and watched the stars float around. He soon started to doze, but was abruptly woken up about 90 minutes later by an incoming video transmission.

A young officer in a KSF uniform sat in some kind of operations office, "KSS 1550-V, this is KSF Tixaya Control."

Ximon answered up, "Roger, Tixaya Control, this is KSS 1550-V. Ready to receive."

"KSS 1550-V, looks like you had an exciting first ARC trip. Your initial report was received by Comm Boat several days ago and Command flagged you for follow-up. So, we've duly contacted you as soon as we received your final survey / contact support and your arrival indicator in system. Command Intel wants a sit-down meeting with you as soon as possible. Are you available at 1330 tomorrow?"

Ximon checked his location and time. "Sure, we should hit dirt late tonight, and I can be ready to meet tomorrow. Can you tell me who I'll be meeting with?"

"Roger. I'm showing a Commander Jamison and a few survey techs. Report to Building 3-F, room 2-T."

He radioed Elsbeth, "Elsbeth, looks like we're famous. They want a follow-up meeting tomorrow. Would you care to join me for that?"

"I can if you need me to, but I'd rather pass. I was hoping to be drunk then and you DO get paid the big bucks."

He laughed at that, "I'm not sure I get paid at all. In any case, enjoy your drink, but I guess it's possible this could turn into follow-on meetings."

"Sounds like a blast. By the way, here's the final list of parts. If you just hit 'approve,' I can go ahead and order."

"Sure. Like I said, I may not get paid."

"Boo hoo. Have fun with the big wigs."

Ximon ensured that all his data and both reports were readily available on his tablet. He wasn't entirely sure what to wear. He could still wear his KSF uniform, but ARC members certainly weren't required to. He finally decided this might be his only meeting with big wigs, so he dusted off his uniform and wore that. He got a ride to building 3-F quite early, set up in room 2-T, and waited.

A KSF admin technician came in a few minutes later and got things set up. He also brought in a pitcher of water, so Ximon topped off his water bottle.

Just before the scheduled time, several survey analysts came in and introduced themselves –

Senior Sensor Operator (SSO) Karik and Sensor Operator (SO) Janus. Then Commander (CDR) Jamison arrived and everyone came to attention before being seated. Ximon noted that Jamison didn't take the seat at the head of the table. He wondered what that implied.

CDR Jamison opened the meeting, "This is a review of the KSS SC-1550-V report on Avar 4 and associated incidents. We will start by discussing the deviations from historical data and go from there."

He then motioned to the survey analysts. The lead, Senior Sensor Operator (SSO) Karik, brought up various sensor data on the screen and briefly summarized the historical data on Avar 4. He then said, "... and now this is what LCDR Sabo reports" and summarized some of the highlights Ximon and his team had noted.

CDR Jamison interrupted, "LCDR Sabo, could you summarize your interpretation of these deviations?"

Ximon thought for a moment and then replied. "Certainly. As noted in both the initial and final reports, the deviations appear to stem from intentional terraforming actions changing atmospheric composition and planetary magnetic fields."

"And why did you conclude this was the case?"

"It was the explanation that we felt best accounted for the degree of deviation in such a short period of time. It was then acknowledged, or claimed, as such by The People."

"So you have no definitive proof of terraforming actions?"

"No, we did not have the capability to more fully study the changes in real-time to investigate other avenues. We did not find specific terraforming equipment, but did find an artificial satellite placed by The People to monitor these changes."

"SSO Karik, what is your team's assessment of the planetary changes?"

SSO Karik replied, "Sir, after a detailed review of the two data sets, we came to the same conclusion as LCDR Sabo – that the most likely explanation was intentional terraforming actions."

"Understood. Now let's discuss this satellite. LCDR Sabo, please explain that."

Ximon reviewed his notes and the data showing on the screen. "As noted, while orbiting Avar 4 we detected what appeared to be an artificial satellite orbiting the southern hemisphere. As we conducted subsequent orbital passes, we got closer and did imagery and sensor analysis. We concluded it was an observation satellite of unfamiliar design and that it was periodically transmitting data to a point near the edge of the system."

Jamison paused and seemed to ponder this for a moment. "And please explain the data."

Ximon continued, "We could not initially decipher the data, but eventually concluded that it was likely numeric data on atmospheric conditions, sent periodically in compressed, encrypted bursts toward the point mentioned."

"I see … and please explain this point you refer to."

"We triangulated the apparent transmission arc to an area encompassing a 15-degree arc from Avar 4 planet, 10 to 20 degrees of the orbital plane, to an area 28-30 AU from the sun. The estimated geographic coordinates of the target area are contained in the NOTOSC we issued."

Halfway through that discussion, an elderly man in a civilian suit entered and took the head of the table. CDR Jamison greeted him, "Attaché Brask, welcome. We are just coming to discussion of the aliens." He then pointed to Ximon, "This is LCDR Sabo, the captain of the vessel involved."

Brask nodded to Ximon, glanced briefly at the screens, and said, "We in the Republic Foreign office are quite interested in this apparent first contact situation, in the race described, and in discussions to this point. Please continue."

CDR Jamison did just that, "… and LCDR Sabo, what was located in the region the data was being transmitted to?"

"We assumed it was some kind of vessel monitoring the satellite data remotely. We later learned it contained several vessels."

"Understood. Now please describe your encounter with this 'alien' vessel."

"Very well. After completing cubesat deployments and surveys of Avar 4 and its moons, we prepared to jump from the system. We selected a jump point near the region mentioned in hopes of detecting something. As we headed in that direction, we spotted a vessel at long range. It was on very nearly an intercept course with us, accelerating at a speed nearly identical to ours."

"Continue."

"We attempted to initiate contact, but initially only got garbled data bursts akin to the data from the satellite. As we got closer, their transmission refined to the point we could understand them."

Brask interrupted then, "And why did you establish contact?"

"We had what appeared to be an alien vessel on an intercept course. Communication is recommended approach in that situation. Further, we felt we could gain valuable information about the situation and the vessel."

Brask seemed satisfied and said no more.

CDR Jamison motioned with his hand to say, "Continue."

Ximon looked between Jamison and Brask before answering. "Once we could communicate, we identified ourselves and they identified themselves as Planetoid Vessel 7 of 'The People.' They stated that they had found Avar 4 unused, had claimed it for their use, and were actively terraforming it. They asked why we were interfering with their claim.

"We told them that our leaders had claimed this planet and that we had been directed to study why it's changing. They said that it is, of course, changing because they're changing it to be a new home for their people. If we understood what they said and the map they sent us, they've travelled like 17-star systems in 213 years on some kind of generation ship. We told them we're peaceful and will go back and tell our leaders about them.

"Then we told them more about humans and asked about them. They sent us some images and told us they had several ships. We then headed for the jump point while Vessel 7 headed for the planet. We told them to leave the mining stations and shipping alone, and then sent a NOTOSC out for everyone to leave them alone and avoid confrontation. As we neared the jump point, we were met by another alien vessel, #11, who escorted us until we jumped. During that trip, the vessel established a video link so we got the video of them that you see. Finally, just before we jumped, we took a lot of long-range images of their other ships in that comm target area. We noted eight vessels of varying size, at least one of which looked to be a pretty massive planetoid. Then we jumped."

Brask cleared his throat noisily before speaking. "So what did you promise them?"

"What? I didn't promise them anything. I assured them that we wanted peace and that our leaders," he motioned pointing to them "would want to talk to them. We told them that our leaders MIGHT be willing to assist them in some way, but I promised nothing."

Brask continued, "Why did you tell them so much?"

"I did what I understood was appropriate in a first contact situation and keep in mind that I had to worry about the safety of my ship and crew. We were in a small, unarmed survey craft. Both the vessels we encountered were at least 10 times our size and they had a lot more ships. I had to keep them calm while we gathered information and got out of there."

Brask appeared somewhat skeptical or suspicious for a moment, but then his features smoothed. "Very well. As the apparent first contacting officer, what are your recommendations on how we deal with them?

Ximon was afraid they'd ask that and had considered it. "Sir, I recommend sending a small group of ships, establish contact, and possibly establish trade. I feel they'll react violently if you tell them they have to leave the planet."

CDR Jamison dove in, "What makes you think that?"

"They've travelled far and believe they will soon have a home for their children. They also seemed incapable of understanding that we might claim the planet since we weren't using it."

Brask asked, "So what do you, in your expert opinion, believe the Republic should do as far as the planet? You know that the Republic claimed it several decades ago."

"I'm not expert in inter-solar negotiations, but I've heard of cases where the Republic will grant refugees an unused planet if they agree to act as a peaceful protectorate. I believe that could be considered. We might benefit from trade with them."

CDR Jamison looked doubtful. "From what you've described, they sound somewhat primitive. What could they give us?"

"Sir, their long-range travel didn't appear very advanced, but we got little detail about their ship technology overall. Also, their terraforming capabilities appear fairly impressive – they produced fairly dramatic changes quite quickly."

Brask nodded. "The Republic thanks you for your report, for making this first contact, and for successfully completing your mission. If we have further questions for you, we will contact you."

He then turned to Jamison, "The captain's mission appears wholly successful. Please have someone pay him promptly for his service."

Ximon warmed up at that. "Thank you, sir. I have already submitted the paperwork."

Then Brask added one more thing, "Until the Republic has established more formal relations, please closely limit your discussions about The People."

"Of course, sir."

CDR Jamison looked to Brask to ensure he had nothing else and then concluded, "Thank you LCDR Sabo. Ensure your crew is aware of direction to limit discussion on this issue.

Good day."

Ximon left relieved and excited, but also realized he had to reach Elsbeth.

As soon as he got out of the building, he called Elsbeth. It rang several times, but no answer. He tried again with the same result. Finally, on the third try, she answered. She was clearly in a loud place, like a bar, and she was also fairly drunk. "Hey Ximon, you calling to cure my nightmares?"

He started speaking several times, but it was clear she couldn't hear. Eventually, he pretty much needed to yell for her to hear. "Elsbeth, I've got to talk to you. Where are you?"

"I'm in a bar. I told you I was getting drunk."

"Understood, but WHICH bar?"

Elsbeth's speech was pretty slurred. "The Purple something.....uh, uh, the something Pilot."

"The Purple Pilot?"

"That might be it. Do you like it?"

"If that's it, I'm on my way. STAY THERE?"

"I ain't going nowhere. They've got good drinks and a decent band."

Ximon quickly got a ride and asked for the Purple Pilot. The robocab said, "I do not show an address entry for the Purple Pilot. Here's a list of several establishments that contain the word "Purple." Do you see the appropriate one?"

There were many establishments of many types.

"Just show me bars!"

"Yes, sir, the only bar entry I show with the term Purple in the name is the Purple Pigeon. Will that do?"

"Yes, take me there ... and fast."

The Purple Pigeon was a place that looked like it had once been nice ... probably a long time ago. There were lots of prostitutes hanging around outside, the music was loud, and the neighborhood was sleazy. Ximon paid his cover and headed in.

The place was dark and filled with scented vapor. Dozens of drunks sat at the bar or in booths. He walked around trying to find Elsbeth. He found her at the bar, listing visibly, and dressed like she didn't plan to go home alone, but she was nursing a drink badly.

She lit up when she saw Ximon and slurred out, "Hey look guys, this is my friend Ximon. He thinks I'm hot. I don't know what's wrong with you guys."

"Elsbeth, let's get out of here. I need to talk to you."

"You just want to get in my pants, don't you?"

Ximon hesitated and considered what to say, but finally said, "Sure, whatever you want, but let's get out of here."

"I can't leave now, I'm got a whole drink here." She looked at her drink and saw that it was pretty well empty. "Well, I need a drink."

"Elsbeth, come with me and I'll buy you a bottle of whatever you want."

"I told you, you're just trying to take advantage of me."

"I won't take advantage of you, but I'll cure your nightmares."

"OK, that would be great. Take me home, sailor. I'm drunk and need to get naked."

He nearly had to carry her out and pour her into the robocab. She started dozing off almost immediately. Ximon realized he didn't know where her apartment was. He tried to ask her, but she just nuzzled his shoulder and drooled a bit. So, he had the cab take them to the ship.

He got her inside with some effort and almost carried her to her room. He started taking some of her clothes off so she could sleep comfortably.

That woke her up a bit, "Oh, baby, they can't keep their hands off me."

Once he had her shoes and shirt off, he nudged her onto the bed, and she rolled over fast asleep. He debated whether to go to his room, but figured she might need supervision, so he climbed in bed next to her and went to sleep. She was sick in the night and spent some time in the bathroom. When she climbed back into bed, she snuggled up to him and started snoring.

He woke up and got breakfast in the galley. She joined him, looking pretty rough in ragged sweats, "What the hell happened last night? Did you get me drunk?"

"No, Elsbeth, you got yourself well and truly drunk. I came and rescued you."

"Oh, and then took me right to bed I see. I'm not complaining, but some would call that taking advantage."

"Elsbeth, I was the perfect gentleman and just kept you company."

She feigned offense at that and yelled, "That's even worse! How could you?"

He got her some food and some coffee.

After she downed quite a bit of both she said, "So how'd your thing go?"

"That's what I needed to talk to you about. It seemed to go OK, but they don't want us to talk about it until they figure out what to do."

"You know me" she said, patting her stomach, "as tight as a drum. I wouldn't say anything." Then she got a faraway look. "Well, I guess I did say something to a few guys at the bar, but they were just interested in my body."

"I'm sure they were. Hey, I'm sorry to have pulled you away from all that glamor, but I was worried about you."

"… and the talking thing."

Ximon nodded. "And the talking thing."

Ximon explained everything that had been discussed and said he hoped they'd be paid quickly. He also told her that she could order those parts as soon as she wanted.

She nodded like it hurt to do so. "Yeah, that's great. I'll do that later today, but now I'm going home and getting some sleep. I couldn't sleep with you pawing all over me. I'll see you tomorrow." She ended with a wink and left the ship to get a cab.

Ximon shook his head in dismay. Then he decided maybe he needed a nap and asked Raiza to join him in his room.

He awoke a few hours later and, true to form, Raiza had washed all his clothes and laid out fresh ones. She had also made a nice lunch for him in bed. He thanked her and said, "Raiza, you are a great comfort."

She said somewhat sultrily, "You are always welcome Ximon. I love to serve you."

After a nice lunch, he got on the computer to look on ScoutLink. He was planning to look for potential next jobs and possibly another crew member. However, as soon as he got online, he saw he had a couple messages.

First, he had an invoice for the job. The job was worth 30,000 CR, but he'd been paid 64,000 CR. The document accompanying it explained that he was paid for the job, plus a bonus for additional information and first contact, plus a small fee for post-mission consultation. The message also had non-disclosure agreements for both him and Elsbeth to sign.

"Well, sweet, I can pay Elsbeth, buy those parts, and still have a chunk of money."

He immediately sent Elsbeth her salary, plus a bonus for additional work. He also sent her the contract documents again and offered her a small signing bonus. At present, he could afford to be generous. He also told her, let me know how much you will need to hire a maintenance assistant for a few days.

He also had a message from KSF ARC Control thanking him for his mission completion and pointing him to the job board to consider more opportunities to serve. That was nice, since he was planning to go there anyway.

Next, rather than scrolling through people on Scout Link, he posted a job offering. He was asking for applicants with Scout Survey Operator / Scientist experience, preferably also with some lesser experience in Navigation or Engineering. He offered a monthly contract and clearly indicated the initial plan was to take KSF ARC jobs.

Then he looked at a few ship components he hadn't discussed with Elsbeth, specifically a turret and weapons. Offensive weapons were too expensive, but he found a used refurbished turret that would fit and bought it and a basic chaff thrower (defensive anti-laser weapon) to go in it. He just hadn't liked being totally "naked" out there. He was sure that Elsbeth would be thrilled at installing it.

He bought upgraded navigation, scanner, and translation software packages for the Mantis computer. He restocked the galley and bought some miscellaneous other supplies. This included replacing a couple old vacc suits, adding a few additional air tanks, and stocking the small weapons locker with a shotgun and a few pistols.

He also sent Raiza to TSR for a "reluster." This was sort of like a spa day for a companion bot. They basically treated her 'skin' with deep moisturizer that restored its flexibility and suppleness. Then they treated her hair, replacing some, recoloring it to its intended shade, and super moisturizing it. Finally, they did a full maintenance check and tune up. They even installed slight upgrades to her voice processing software and some "companion" routines.

After all, what good captain doesn't take care of the whole crew?

Ximon spent some time just strolling around the city, but mainly hung out around the ship. Over the next several days, Elsbeth and a middle-aged mechanic fixed a bunch of stuff on the ship – the arm, some tuning stuff she hadn't gotten to, and LOTS of minor wiring things. She was NOT thrilled that Ximon had bought a turret without consulting her, but they got that mounted and got the chaff thrower in case. It wasn't much, but it was SOMETHING. She didn't sleep on the ship (as he did), but she showed up every morning and left late every afternoon. Only occasionally did she appear hungover when she came in and she did great work regardless.

During that, he got several inquiries about the job opening and examined their profiles. He rejected a few out of hand as too inexperienced, but three candidates looked promising: a) Idayvo Oretes - a 30-ish year old guy with skin so black Ximon couldn't make out details from the photo; b) Scott Jacobs - a retired guy pushing 60; and C) Ekh-agh-gaen an actual Canid. The latter was interesting -- Canid are a substantial minority within the Republic, but they tended to be concentrated closer to the areas bordering Canid space. He decided to interview all of them via video call rather than his "coin toss" like last time. He also invited Elsbeth to participate to get an additional perspective and because they might have some maintenance role.

The interviews went fine. All seemed to have reasonable experience. Idayvo Oretes had some good, recent survey/analysis expertise, and a little experience in gunnery, ground operations, and navigation. However, his survey experience was all on newer vessels with newer sensors than Mantis. Scott Jacobs was kind of the opposite issue. He had extensive survey experience on older classes of ships such as the Vanguard, but most of his experience was a decade or more old. He also had a little maintenance experience, but that too was decades old. Ekh-agh-gaen was quite interesting. He appeared to have solid skills, had recent survey experience and a little training in pilot and navigation, but it wasn't clear when he'd be available.

It was clear that Elsbeth was watching the interview calls while working. She didn't ask a lot or provide a lot of commentary, but she later seemed to favor Idayvo, who was Ximon's #1 as well. His experience was substantial and varied, with useful expertise aside from sensor operations, and he just seemed to be the best fit temperament-wise. So Ximon offered the job to him. He excitedly accepted and said he could sign on in a week. He had a few things to arrange first. He also told them they could call him "Iday" so that was a bit easier.

Then Ximon got to work on finding their next gig.

JAUNT 2: LITTLE LOST SHEEP

Scoutlink showed quite a few ARC jobs, but Ximon's criteria ruled many out because they were too soon, too far in the future, or required a larger ship and/or crew than he had. He bid on two jobs. One was relatively nearby (three jumps this time) and required only some basic surveying, followed by some investigation on the ground. All the crew's contracts included going on ground missions as necessary, so he felt OK about signing on for that. The other job appeared to just be a simple scan job and would only require one extra jump from the end of first job, so he applied for that as well. Soon, they were signed up to do both starting the next week.

Iday signed on board and greeted Ximon warmly, "Captain, thank you again for this opportunity. I look forward to serving aboard the Mantis."

Iday was tall and fairly skinny, just under two meters tall, with very dark skin, and very short hair. He travelled light, carrying just a duffel bag and a small backpack. He wore some basic grey utility clothing and wore an infinity symbol on a breakaway chain around his neck. After chatting for a few minutes, he got settled into a cabin.

Then he and Ximon spent several hours going over the Mantis' sensors, getting him access, etc. Then Iday did some diligent sensor study and testing on his own. He also briefly examined the navigation computer and the fire control for the turret.

A few hours later, Ximon called everyone together and said they'd take off in two days to do two missions, totaling six to eight weeks. Iday met everyone, including Raiza and the

Mantis AI. He greeted Raiza like any woman and was polite to Mantis. It seemed very likable and it seemed like he'd fit in well.

Ximon briefed the crew on the mission. "OK, we'll take off day after tomorrow around 0800. We've got two missions. The first one is to investigate a Scout outpost on Cybex Beta 3. KSF has lost contact with the team there and our job is to find out why and take some scans and ground observations. We'll jump to the Tidaya system, skim, jump to the Propelis system, skim, and then jump to our destination -- Cybex Beta. There, we'll skim, go in to Cybex Beta 3, do some scans, land, investigate a Scout outpost there, and do some ground observations. When we're done there, it's just one additional jump to the Moda system where we'll take some components to the Scout station there and do a moderately near pass of Moda Sol and some refresh scans of Moda 1. Then back here past a few intermediate jump points. Any questions?"

Elsbeth said, "Can we at least stop at the station at Propelis 7? It's almost halfway, would give us a chance to stretch our legs, possibly resupply, and they've got a few good restaurants, shows, and bars there."

"Possibly. I'll have to check how far out of our way it is and whether there are any advisories. More than anything else, it'll depend on how we're doing otherwise. Anything else?"

Iday raised his hand, "Captain, can you tell us more about this ground work on Cybex Beta?"

"It's Ximon. I'm still studying some of the details, but it appears the team there basically 'fell off the grid.' The KSF has no idea what happened to them, wants to know about them, and wants an update on what they were working on, which was doing ground observations of some local creatures. As I understand it, we'll need to land a way off, air raft to near the outpost, hike the last little way, investigate the outpost, and then stay there for a couple of days for observations."

Elsbeth piped up, "Hiking? How far are we talking?"

"As I said, I'm still studying the details, but it looks like three to four kilometers. Nothing that'll break our backs. I'll send y'all the mission summary a little later."

"Well, I guess I'd better do some more checks on the air raft – I don't want to have to walk the entire way. Iday could you help me with that once we're in jump?"

Iday seemed a bit surprised to be addressed, but nodded. "Of course, though I can't purport to be an expert."

"I just need a hand."

"Very well. Just let me know."

Seeing that everything seemed planned, Ximon concluded. "OK. I'll see y'all in the morning, just before 0800. I'll ask Raiza to make us breakfast."

They all gathered, chatted a bit, and ate the breakfast Raiza had put together.

Elsbeth got up, "Well, I want to make a few quick checks before takeoff. Thanks for breakfast."

Iday nodded in a faint bow of sorts. "Yes, thank you for the hospitality. Thank you, Raiza. If you don't mind, I'll stow my things and then join you on the bridge, Ximon."

"Please do. I'm sure you've seen it more than a few times, but I want you to watch how the process plays out here and then I'd like you to take some practice scans on some of the objects we pass heading for the jump point."

"That is exactly what I wished to do if time allowed. I'll be on the bridge in ten minutes."

Ximon settled in to his seat, did some pre-checks, and had Mantis do some pre-checks. Everything looked good. So, as soon as Iday was settled, Ximon asked for clearance to leave and took off.

The flight out of system was uneventful and Iday seemed

to know what he was doing. Ximon also had him independently calculate a jump solution to ensure he could work the Nav system. Iday's solution was quite close to Ximon, so he did have some knowledge there.

They jumped and that, too, was uneventful.

During the jump, Elsbeth did a lot of work on the Air Raft, with some help from Iday. She was NOT impressed, but she felt confident it wouldn't fall out of the sky at the first chance. Except when he was helping Elsbeth or doing some additional refresher training on ship systems, Iday spent a lot of time in his quarters or reading in the common room.

On the fifth day in jump, Elsbeth caught Ximon at breakfast and launched into him in mock indignation, "Ximon, I was hoping you'd hire a hot boy toy and Iday's close enough for me, but I can't believe you hired a PRIEST!"

"I do remember something from his profile about attending a seminary, but I didn't notice he was ordained."

"He IS ordained and it's in some religion that preaches self-improvement, kindness, and CELIBACY of its priests until they are DIRECTED to marry a member of their congregation. What kind of companionship is he going to be for me?"

"As you know, Iday looked like the best candidate. Would you rather the retiree that's 10-15 years older than us, or," he smirked, "perhaps you were hoping for some 'puppy love' with the Canid, eh?"

Elsbeth groaned and punched him in the shoulder.

So, he continued, "… and as far as companionship, he may be outstanding at songs, games, stories, gospel discussions, etc. He might be the most enlightening companion you've ever had." Then he put his hand on his own chest, "Present company excluded, of course."

She groaned in exasperation, "MEN!" and stalked off.

"Be nice to him ... and be nice to me."

She looked back at him as she left the galley, "Yeah, you wish."

The rest of the jump was uneventful. Iday did prove to be quite good at some of the games they did have in the galley computer table, but he was a terrible singer. He was also quite willing to help Elsbeth in Engineering or Ximon on the bridge. When not doing any of those things, he was doing scripture study or taking classes in his room. Elsbeth spent a lot of time in Engineering and, otherwise, watched vids while sipping, or gulping, wine. Ximon did a little of the latter, watched some vids, reviewed the mission notes, and spent some time with Raiza. Some of that was entertainment, but he did work with her on donning and testing vacc suits.

They came out at Tidaya and all was well. They ran in, skimmed fuel at the gas giant, ran out, and jumped again. Total time about 20 hours. Ximon was getting used to applying more Gs of acceleration and he, Mantis, and the crew all seemed to do OK with it.

The jump to Propelis was also perfectly boring. They jumped in past Propelis 8 and ran there to skim. While doing so Ximon announced, "Crew, we're ahead of schedule so we're going to take a few hours to visit the station at Propelis station. We can be on station for about 12 hours."

Elsbeth grumbled, "Well, THERE'S a shocker." She then paused, smiled, and said, "Thanks."

They docked at the Propelis 7 station without incident (though not without a fee). The station was on the planet's main moon and focused on mining, some trade, and entertainment. The "permanent" population was about 200,000, but there were usually several thousand visitors at any given time. It wasn't exactly "civilization," but it did have some decent places and sometimes just stretching your legs was enjoyable.

They were all in the bridge as they docked talking about options and looking at the ads streaming to their comms. They agreed to head to dinner, eat, and then separate from there. Ximon was going to do a little shopping, Elsbeth wanted to hit a concert at a bar, and Iday wanted to see "the sights" (the views of the moon) and visit his church. They had a real nice meal and off they went with Ximon reminding them before they broke up, "It's 1900, be back on the ship" then he looked at Elsbeth and emphasized, "CONSCIOUS by 0600 so we can get moving." She just rolled her eyes and waved over her shoulder as she left, drink in hand.

It was a nice night. Ximon hit several stores, got some treats for the ship, and bought some trinkets. He also bought himself some clothes and bought some for Raiza (unlike some companion bot owners, he DID keep her clothed … most of the time). She thanked him profusely for his kindness and they had a good night.

In the morning, he was on the bridge and anxious to leave by 0530. Iday had spent the night in the ship and came to the bridge around the same time.

Ximon asked Mantis, "Did Elsbeth return to the ship?"

"No, captain, nor have I received any communications from her."

When she wasn't there by 0545, Ximon called her, but got no answer. He directed Mantis to keep contacting her every five minutes until she arrived. He got more frustrated as 0600 approached. He and Iday did pre-checks and Mantis reported all was well with the ship. At 0615 Mantis informed Ximon that Elsbeth was approaching. He had Iday continue with pre-flight while he met Elsbeth in the galley.

Elsbeth was clearly tipsy and looked like she had either slept in her clothes or been in and out of them. But she wasn't horribly drunk and appeared to be rushing. When she saw him, she said (as if it was nothing), "Woops, sorry. I had a great time."

Her nonchalance was just the thing to set him off, so he tore into her. "I agreed to come here because YOU suggested it and then I set back our take off time about an hour so we'd have a little more time, but you … YOU … couldn't just get back here on time anyway. And then, to top it off, you couldn't call to let us know where you were at or bother to answer our calls. Did you lose your comm unit? Drop it in a toilet or something? Or did you just not give a damn that we were sitting here waiting?"

His anger seemed to wake her up and she got defensive. "Ximon, I was only a few minutes late."

"I guess when you retired, you retired your ability to be reliable in the process. This is crap. You treated us like crap. Now, if you're not too drunk to read a gauge, get down to Engineering, strap your happy ass in, and watch things while we take off … NOW!"

She huffed off as Ximon stalked back to the bridge saying, "Taking off in five minutes. We'll be doing a 3G burn to the jump point to make up time."

Ximon was very quiet as they headed for the jump point. The sustained high Gs kept them all seated and uncomfortable. He didn't hear a word from Elsbeth. However, it seemed like Iday (who could obviously see the tension), asked both of them mundane questions in an apparent effort to calm tensions. Ximon reflected that apparently Iday DID have some conflict resolution skills. Ximon had him calculate the jump solution and then went over it with him while making some minor calculations. He hadn't considered quite all the gravitational fields on both ends of the jump that he should have, but the Nav computer probably would have factored most of that in automatically.

They jumped without incident and had several more days of lull. After a day or two Elsbeth seemed to have stopped hiding and was seen around a bit more. Finally, on the third day, she caught Ximon in the galley and launched right in, "Ok, Ximon, I got it – I screwed up. I was anxious to blow off some steam and have some fun, I got pretty drunk, got a little lucky, and stopped paying attention. Then I didn't want to deal with your calls when I already knew I was going to be late. That was stupid and childish. I'm sorry. I can only guarantee it won't happen again."

Ximon had mellowed a bit too. "Understood, but it can't happen again – I need to be able to count on you. We all need to be able to count on each other."

She nodded and said, "I totally agree. It's been a while since I've had anyone to count on or who would count on me."

"So, we're good but, Elsbeth, you have to know you have a drinking problem. You've got to deal with it so it's not a problem on the job."

She looked a bit abashed but nodded.

Then Ximon continued, "You know, you honestly might consider talking to Iday about it. I don't know about his religion, but a lot of preachers have training in dealing with this kind of stuff."

She looked skeptical. "I'll think about it, but I don't really want to discuss my personal life with my crew."

Ximon smiled a bit at the absurdity of that. "You already are right now, and you might laugh, but if you don't want to talk to Iday, you can talk to Mantis – the computer has a bunch of self-help type routines, so Scouts don't fall apart out here. Failing that, I'm sure you can find some vids or programs on the net."

She nodded as she left and then stopped in the doorway, "Ximon, I won't screw this up again."

To which he nodded and smiled.

As the jump went on, Ximon called the crew together and

laid out the plan. He showed some maps of where the outpost was, showed the closest the mission said they could land to the outpost, and then where they'd have to fly and hike. He showed blueprints of the outpost and summaries of the crew that should be there – two males and two female scouts specializing in scientific analysis. He also provided a planetary breakdown of Cybex Beta 3 and some info on the local creatures they were observing.

Cybex Beta 3:

> *Diameter: 15,000 km*
> *Surface Water: 75%*
> *Distance from sun: 0.9 AU*
> *Atmosphere: Oxygen/nitrogen, non-toxic*
> *Gravity: 1.1 G*
> *Temperature Range: -45 to 48 C*
> *Lifeforms:*
> > *- Heavy vegetation - grasslands, some forests*
> > *-Variety of small, furred creatures that appear mammalian*
> > *- Cybexapods - Large omnivores, quadraped, but can also stand on hind legs to gather fruit and leaves from tree-like brush. Construct primitive shelters out of branches.*

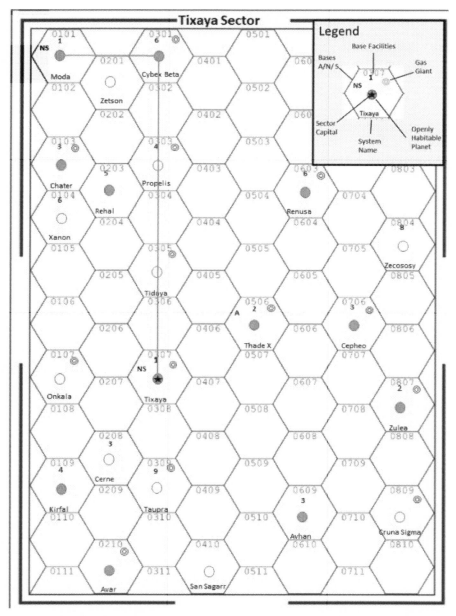

The team had been monitoring various weather phenomenon

and the general environment, but their main focus was on monitoring several large groups of Cybexapods. These large omnivores showed signs of being intelligent, but the team needed to understand their level of intelligence and development to judge whether, or when, some form of contact might be safely conducted or whether the planet should be 'quarantined' so their development wasn't interfered with.

After Ximon briefed the crew he asked for thoughts and concerns.

Iday asked, "I assume we'll take weapons when we go to the surface. The information doesn't say whether those creatures are dangerous, but they're certainly big enough to be ..."

Elsbeth interrupted, "... and we don't know what happened to the team."

Iday continued, unphased, "So, what do we have for weapons?"

Ximon answered, "Well, I'm not sure about y'all, but a good portion of Scouts I've served with have had their own weapons. If you do, that's certainly fine. Failing that, here's our armory ...," and he ticked off on his fingers, "One shotgun, 4 pistols, 4 knives, and a fair amount of ammo. We don't have any armor unless we want to wear vacc suits."

Elsbeth looked with surprised or worried at that. "Are you suggesting we wear vacc suits? The info on the planet says the atmosphere is breathable and non-toxic."

"I was still debating that. The atmosphere IS breathable, but it's thinner than we're used to and a bit thinner yet at the outpost since it's up a few thousand meters."

Iday added, "I guess there's also the possibility of some kind of disease or some dangerous chemical in the air."

Ximon agreed with that. "That IS a possibility to consider, but I'm not sure we need to go complete vacc suits."

"I agree. We could take oxygen tanks in case we need them for the thin air. We'd have some disease or chemical protection if we have our coverall sleeves down, with gloves, and breather or oxygen masks. I'd recommend hats as well. It doesn't look like it'll be too hot. Do we have backpacks?"

"Yes, standard Scout surplus. Of course, if you've got your own, you're welcome to use them, likewise, if you've got your own weapons or armor."

No one did, which surprised him a little.

Ximon continued, "Let's take vacc suits in the air raft, but leave them with the raft and go on as Iday suggests. We'll each wear a breather mask and bring an air tank. Everyone brings a pistol, a pack with at least four liters of water, a light jacket, and at least four REMs (ready-eat-meals). Iday, I'd like you to carry the shotgun and I'll carry the water filter kit and a small tool kit just in case. We'll all have our comm units for taking basic images, but Elsbeth you'll carry the long-range camera. We shouldn't need it because they should have observation gear at the outpost, but who knows."

Then he added, "Raiza, you're our quartermaster for this. I want you to check each of us to ensure we have the necessary supplies. Then, you'll stay with Mantis and monitor our comms. You're our final fallback plan in case we have issues and can't get Mantis to us, but it's a long way from the ship to the outpost on foot – about 30 kilometers."

Raiza responded, "As you wish, Captain. If necessary, I can walk any distance to assist, though my performance across rough terrain is sub-optimal."

"Thanks, Raiza, but I hope it won't come to that." While Raiza's body did mimic human motion, it wasn't really designed for extended walking on rough terrain. It was assumed that bots of her type would mainly be walking around a home, a ship, or on a night out on the town.

"Mantis, you'll monitor our comms too and basically keep things buttoned up. I'll pre-program a flight path that you can follow that'll bring you a lot closer to the outpost in case things really go bad and we can signal you if we need you to land somewhere else."

Mantis replied, "Roger, Captain. In normal conditions I can land on any flat surface approximately 10,000 meters square."

Finally Ximon added, "OK, so have your packs put together as we discussed and stowed in the galley before we come out of jump. We'll add the weapons after we skim. Any other thoughts anyone?"

Everyone just kind of nodded, so they went about their jump-time pastimes. Ximon watched some training videos, did a little reading, and spent time with Raiza. Elsbeth liked to drink and watch trashy videos in her quarters or, occasionally, in the common room. Iday studied ship systems studiously and spent a lot of time reading his holy books or watching religious videos, usually in his room. All of them also got to know one another better. Iday was, indeed, an ordained priest in his religion, but he had no congregation to tend so he was able to work and continue his studies until he was called to one. He was good company – a good conversationalist showing great interest in everyone else. He also never seemed judgmental or pressured any of them on his religion.

A few days later Mantis came out of jump with Ximon, Iday, and Elsbeth all on the bridge. They were out near the Cybex Beta 5 orbit and headed for the Beta 5 gas giant to skim. Iday did long-range system scans as they headed in. He detected a tramp freighter with 2 shuttles deployed for skimming (since the ship wasn't aerodynamic enough to skim) at the gas giant as they approached.

Ximon hailed them with their transponder code, raising

his eyebrows at their name. "Scow 785, this is Captain Sabo of the KSS Survey Craft Mantis on a survey mission to Beta 3. Please state your mission here."

"Mantis, this is Captain Brax of the Scow. We're just a light freighter passing through for enough gas to get home. As soon as we bring these shuttles in, we'll be heading for our jump point."

"Roger Scow. Have you detected any other ships or anomalous activity in the system?"

"Nope. Quiet and boring. That's much as we like it."

"Sounds good, Scow. Have a good flight. Mantis out."

Iday and Mantis noted nothing else of interest and the skimming was without incident.

As they neared Beta 3, Ximon directed Mantis to do continuous baseline scans, while Iday did targeted atmospheric and meteorological scans. He also had Mantis continue to try to raise the Scout Outpost, but she got no reply and detected no other electro-magnetic signals. If nothing else, there should have been a beacon from the outpost sending station status messages, but nothing.

Mantis noted, "Captain, they have a comm relay in geo-synchronous orbit in the arc above the outpost. I have interrogated it for messages using the command codes provide in the mission tasking, but the relay has received no signals from the planet for 27 days."

They entered orbit and circled for about 12 hours, updating their mapping data and monitoring for any activity.

They confirmed their landing site and brought Mantis in for landing. The terrain approximated Terran-normal (the baseline they used for comparison), but with a darker atmosphere and a greyish green tint to the vegetation. They landed in a small valley near grasslands and met in the galley. As Ximon had directed, Raiza went down a mental checklist of gear with each of them and verified the pressure in their oxygen tanks.

Elsbeth had pre-flighted the air raft. She said wryly, "The raft's as good to go as it's going to be."

The air raft was nothing so much as an old, convertible ground vehicle, but without wheels. It used some minimal anti-gravity capability, supplemented by vented engines, to maintain some altitude, and had small reaction engines that were largely sealed so they could work in a variety of atmospheres and densities. It had four seats and a small "bed" where they could stow gear. Raiza had already placed some extra air, water, and food in there, so by the time they got their packs and vacc suits in, it was fairly full.

Ximon drove and Iday monitored the basis sensors up front. Elsbeth sat in the back so she was close to engine access in case something went wrong.

Before they pulled out of the cargo bay Ximon directed, "Mantis, shut the hatch after we pull out and activate ship defense weapons (there were 3 small weapons mounted near the main ramp and air locks to repel boarders), but prepare for the possibility that other humans could appear in case that scout team is wandering around somewhere. Raiza, don't let anyone but us in without direction from us."

They echoed, near simultaneously, "Roger, Captain. Standing by."

Then they pulled out and took off.

Elsbeth reminded Ximon, "She can theoretically reach about 200 knots and one kilometer in this atmosphere, but I'd recommend we stay low and don't exceed 100 knots, both so we're less likely to be seen and in case she falls out of the sky."

"Very comforting. I'll stay at about 30 meters and wasn't planning to go more than 60 knots or so."

"With the top on, she should have enough air pressure

that we won't feel the effects of the thin air until we get out, but I'll watch that."

Iday played with the scanner controls. "I'll continue scanning and will occasionally hail the outpost. I guess it's possible that something is wrong with their comms."

As they flew, the scenery was interesting -- grasslands, a few forest areas, and some rocky hills. They tried to stay close to rougher terrain, but they saw (and were seen by) some groups of creatures that matched the images of the cybexapods, as well as some other grazers and some smaller creatures scurrying about. They saw a few bat-like flying creatures, but not many and none got anywhere near the air raft.

They landed on a flat plateau on the "back side" of the hills that the outpost was on and got out, putting on their breathers and air tanks as they did so. Ximon contacted Mantis, "Mantis, we have landed safely. We'll be in touch."

Elsbeth directed the air raft's primitive AI to alert and send her comm unit video if any creatures approached.

They hiked about one kilometer to a pass around the nearest hill and then another two kilometer toward the stated entrance to the outpost, a tunnel away from the face of the plateau it was on/in. They kept signaling as they went, but got no response and noted no outpost beacon.

After a bit of a scramble up the back of the hill, they found a door recessed in a shallow cave. It was a fairly sturdy door such as one might find on an outside shelter, and it had a key pad next to it.

Ximon shrugged visibly. "Well, I guess we'll knock and see who's home," and pressed the signal button on the pad. The screen came on, showing that the system was on, but they got no response. Ximon also noted that there was, of course, a camera in the keypad, so someone could see them. Yet, after waiting a couple minutes and ringing several times, they got no answer.

Elsbeth quipped, "Well, naturally, the easy way didn't work. What's the plan now?"

"Well, we could assume they've just gone out for lunch and will be back soon, but that doesn't appear likely. Elsbeth, can you see if there's a way to override the key pad and open it?"

Elsbeth stepped up with her tablet. "I'll look. The command codes should let us in, but it depends on the state they left it in." She got a connection to the key pad and started communicating with it. "Well, it's in a locked state, so it's intentional. Let me see." She punched a lot of things on her tablet and said, "Come on, baby," as she waited.

Finally, a light on the panel turned green and she said, "We're in. Thank you, command codes."

Ximon pulled out his pistol. Just before opening the door, he said, "Weapons out, just in case."

Inside the tunnel was only dimly illuminated, but it stretched for many meters through the hill. Ximon signaled Mantis, "Mantis, we're entering the access tunnel. We may have limited comms for a bit."

Then he put on a head lamp and moved forward with Iday trailing on his left and Elsbeth a bit farther back on his right.

After going a bit, he removed his air mask for a minute to shout. "Scout Outpost, we're from the KSF Mantis. We're here to check on you." He got no reply, so he put his mask back on and they kept on going.

After several hundred meters the tunnel branched with a thin, unlock door on each. Ximon double-checked the schematics on this tablet and pointed down the hallway. "OK, the main outpost is straight ahead. This offshoot goes to another overlook spot and their landing pad. Let's go to the main and then we can go from there."

After a few hundred meters more, they came to another

locked, heavy door and key pad that looked like the main outpost door. They tried the same process, but it was again locked from the inside. Again, Elsbeth was able to get it unlocked with the command codes. However, when Ximon tried to open the door, it was clear it was blocked by something heavy beyond.

"Someone, or something, has the door blocked from inside. Iday, give me a hand and let's see if we can shove it in."

They got in position and shoved. Whatever was blocking it was clearly heavy. They got it open six to eight centimeters when two shots rang out from inside. One clanged heavily on the door, while the other struck the wall inside the room beyond the door. Ximon and Iday ducked down against the door quickly and pulled back out their guns. Ximon yelled, "What the hell?"

Then a frantic voice rang out from inside. "One more step and I'll take your heads off, whatever you are. I'm not going down like the others."

Ximon shouted in reply, "I'm LCDR Ximon Sabo from the KSF Mantis. The KSF has sent us here to help you. Put down your weapon and let us in so we can talk this over."

"Oh, sure. I ain't dumb. I see you've got weapons and I don't know you. You've shown you're pretty crafty, so I ain't falling for it."

"Ok, ok, but at least tell us who we're talking to. Like I said, my name's Ximon. My friends out here are Iday and Elsbeth. We're here to help you. Our ship is sitting a couple kilometers away."

"I think you know dang well who I am. You already killed Dowling and Al-Mufti and you ran Lu off. Go away – I don't want no more nonsense."

The team crouched down on the other side of the heavy, solid door.

Elsbeth whispered, "Sounds like he's batty. All we need -- a crazy guy with a gun."

Iday said, "Let me try something." He played with his comm unit and then quickly stuck it out so just the camera extended past the edge of the door.

A shot rang out from inside, but Iday got the phone back in time.

"Let's see what we got."

Iday pulled up the image on his tablet so they could look at it. It was a bit blurry and didn't get them the whole room, but it helped. The room was a common room for relaxation, gathering, etc.

Ximon compared the image/video to the schematics on his tablet. "Ok, that looks like the galley off on the right and there's a door heading off to some of the room on the right. Looks like a pile of furniture against the door."

Then Iday said, "and that's him sitting in a chair directly opposite the door, gun in hand, with a door behind him."

Ximon added, "We can't see it but, per the schematics, there's another door off to the left. Also, the names the guy mentioned check out – they were the rest of the team that was here."

Ximon yelled to the guy, "So, I take it you're Jaylan Zaitsev then, right?"

"Yeah, that's me. What, are you reading my mind now?"

"No, Jaylan, I'm just looking at the file the KSF gave me when they asked us to come here. Can you tell me what happened here?"

"You know I don't believe you're KSF right? You're one of them."

"One of who, Jaylan?"

"Those annoying little guys."

Iday whispered then, "He does sound very disturbed – paranoid and, perhaps, hallucinatory. He could obviously be quite dangerous."

Ximon said, "Yeah, but we've got to try to get him to talk to us."

Then he yelled in, "Jaylan, can you tell me what happened to Carla? Carla Dowling? How did she die?"

Jaylan, "You know better than me. I was here and she was out there with you buggers. One of you tripped her, she hit her head, and died."

"Sorry to hear that, Jaylan. When did that happen?"

"I don't know. A couple of weeks ago maybe? Don't you guys tell time?"

"Thanks Jaylan. Now what about Fauod, Fauod Al-Mufti. What happened to him?"

"Dang it. You know this one too. He came back here after Carla died and you guys shot him somehow, a few days after Carla."

"I'm terribly sorry to hear that Jaylan. Do you have their bodies, or did you bury them Jaylan?"

Another shot rang out and Jaylan yelled, "I'm sick of answer these dang questions. You're just trying to trick me."

"Sorry, Jaylan, we're trying to figure out what happened. Do you have enough food and water?"

"Sure I do. You know this place has a healthy supply."

"Sure, Jaylan, but sometimes they go fast. Just wanted to make sure you have enough water. I know how thirsty it can get."

Iday nodded and whispered to Ximon, "You're trying to make him thirsty, aren't you?"

"I figured it was worth a try." Then he tossed a water bottle in through the door. However, he tossed it straight through the opening, so it rolled over by the galley. That put it where they could see it while still protected by the door.

"Ok, Jaylan, can you tell me about Lu, Humaira Lu. You said she was run off. What happened?"

"You know that too. Somehow you ran her off. She took the shuttle and left me here all alone so you and your buddies could get me and if you don't, I'll just rot."

They heard some rustling in the room and saw Jaylan come over to get the water. He aimed his gun in the general direction of the door but didn't seem to even be looking. They could have shot him through the gap in the door, but had no interest in that. Jaylan was a moderately heavy-set man in filthy coveralls who looked quite haggard. He got the water and then went back and sat down.

"Jaylan, what we'd like to do is take you back to a KSF base. You know that Moda is nearby. We'd take you back to our ship and then take you to the base on Moda. Would you like to go to Moda?"

"Moda would be great, but all you're going to do is take me to my grave."

"Ok, well, they're going to miss you on Moda. They were asking about you. One question before we go … what happened to your radio? We've been trying to call you."

"You know dang well what happened to my radio. Your lot broke off the antennas and who knows what else."

"Ok, thanks. Well, we'll be out of your hair. We'll let them know on Moda that you've decided to stay here permanently. Good luck with that."

Ximon and the crew then slowly walked back down the tunnel, keeping their guns on the door.

Elsbeth narrowed her eyes at Ximon. "You're not going to just leave him, are you?"

"No, of course not. But I think there's a chance he might come after us. If not, we'll try to sneak back and get in some other way."

They walked until they got to the intersection and this time, they took the turn off.

They had just turned when they heard Jaylan yell, "Hey, you lot can't leave me here."

They were around the corner and he had no cameras or viewing here, so they just waited.

They heard him again, "Hey, get back here!" Then he repeated things like, "I can't believe you'd abandon me," "This is no way to treat a shipmate," etc. as he got closer.

Just before they reached the corner, Iday and Ximon came around the corner with their guns out. Jaylan held his gun, but was clearly somewhat shocked and quickly dropped the gun in dismay or, perhaps, confusion.

Iday quickly picked up the gun while Ximon kept his trained on Jaylan.

Ximon motioned back down the hallway with his pistol. "Ok, Jaylan, we're going to go back to your room to talk and look around a bit."

"But, you said you were going to Moda. What about that?"

"We'll go there, but we've got to do some looking around here first."

"You're going to regret it. They'll kill you."

"We'll be careful."

"You'll be dead!"

They took Jaylan back to his room and sat him at the table. One of them kept an eye on him while he quickly downed an entire bottle of something that Elsbeth "just happened" to have in her pack "for medicinal purposes."

Then they looked around and took turns watching him until he passed out. They tied his hands and tied him to a bed in a nearby room. Then they looked around.

The place was a mess, with empty food boxes around and furniture out of place. There were several small crew quarters, the common room they'd seen, a pantry room, another storage room, and then the observation room. There were remnants of crewmate belongings around and Elsbeth started digging through those while they looked at the observation room. It had a 270-degree picture window that overlooked the plain, multiple telescopes, and big cameras. There were several chairs, a couch, a couple end tables, and a little fridge. It WAS a great view. They could see quite a few of the cybexapods, including clumps of several dozen gathering stuff from the tree-like brush. There was also a door leading to a trail along the hill top.

Ximon called Elsbeth. "Are you OK down there? We're going to step outside for a minute."

"Sure, our boy is still sleeping and tied up and I locked the front door. When you get back in, let's compare notes."

Ximon and Iday went out the door and along the trail a way, it went over to another hill top with a different view. On top was basically a crude observation post inside a few bushes. Within the post were a few chairs and some binoculars and not much else. Next to the post, the trail also led down some rough steps down to a small cleft and then out onto the plain. It appeared they could climb down here to get to the plain without being seen. They took video and pictures, went back inside, and sat down at the table with Elsbeth.

Ximon pointed at some papers that Elsbeth was holding. "Ok, what do we got?"

"I found some actual paper research notebooks apparently belonging to Dowling. Most of it looks like gibberish, but the last couple pages talk about she and Al-Mufti hiking down to the plain and then sneaking through the brush for closer observation of some groups of local animals. She mentions that they found fire circles where someone/something was consciously lighting camp fires. But they can't figure out who/what is doing this. The cybexapods show signs of intelligence and crude 'tool use' but nothing like this has been seen among them.

"I also found the station log, apparently maintained by our Sleeping Beauty in there. It starts getting weird about one week before Dowling dies. Jaylan seems convinced that something is intentionally harassing them. Their main antennas were disconnected, they fixed them, and then some of the antennas disappeared! He goes downhill into paranoia fast after Dowling dies and Al-Mufti comes back. He says the little guys got in and shot Al-Mufti, but it seems possible it was an internal conflict borne of paranoia and fear.

"Then it appears that Lu ran off with the shuttle, which this guy blames on the 'little guys' scaring her off. If he did, indeed, kill Al-Mufti, I can well imagine her running for her life, but that doesn't explain what happened to her. Then it sounds like this guy has been locked up in here with no company and no contact, just his fears, for a few weeks – no recipe for sanity."

Ximon dove in, "We just scouted the main observation deck and then found a secondary observation post and a path that Dowling and Al-Mufti apparently used to get a closer look at the natives. What we DIDN'T see was any bodies – Dowling or Al-Mufti. He may have dropped them off the cliff, but it sure would be nice to find one or both."

Iday interjected, "And I think our strongest evidence of what happened is Jaylan. He'll probably wake up soon. When he does, I'd like to try and sit in there with him and see if I can get any more insight or confirmation from him."

Ximon said, "That sounds like a plan and I think I hear him rustling now. Why don't you go in there and maybe take him some food and drink? We'll look around these rooms in more detail while you do so. Everyone, remember to keep your cameras on."

Iday nodded, grabbed some food, headed in, and closed the door behind him.

Ximon and Elsbeth wandered around, took a lot of images, and did a more complete search in all the rooms. They gathered a few items from each team members – comm units, tablets, uniforms, etc. as evidence. However, when Ximon was raiding the large pantry he made a disturbing discovery, "Elsbeth, get in here."

She ducked in and Ximon pointed to a frozen body propped up in the corner behind some boxes in the freezer – this was clearly Al-Mufti, and it was clear he was shot at least twice.

"We're going to have to haul him back to the ship"

Elsbeth acted surprised. "You mean we have to haul a dead guy around for the next month or so?"

"You know we do, though it won't be that long. We'll drop him off at Moda in a week or so."

They searched around more while Iday tried to get Jaylan to talk.

After a while Elsbeth grabbed Ximon's arm and pulled him toward a screen. "I think I found something you should see."

Elsbeth had run all the video footage that the team, especially Dowling, had taken through her tablet. Now she showed Ximon something.

"OK, there's hundreds of hours of this stuff. I'm sure

someone ELSE will find it interesting, but I focused on the footage that was NOT shot here. This clip here is from down that staircase outside."

She played a clip where Al-Mufti is leading Dowling down the trail while the latter films. Something small and hard, like a rock, flew down from the brush and hit Dowling on the shoulder. This was followed by many more such projectiles striking near her and Al-Mufti. They both started to run, Dowling fell, and the camera was covered with blood splatter as Al-Mufti ran away. So, this looked like it might be the death scene for Dowling.

Ximon looked unimpressed. "Interesting and useful, but we still don't know what's going on."

Elsbeth held up a finger as she moved and manipulated the video, "Ah, but look closely right HERE" and she stopped the image. It was during the rock attack and for just a moment the image captured one of the attackers. In one of the shrubs was one of the planet's smaller life forms – about a meter tall, furry, and upright with powerful legs, agile little arms, and a substantial tail, it looked to Ximon a bit like a kangaroo, but somewhat taller and with more substantial arms. It was standing in the brush. holding some kind of stick (like an ancient spear thrower) and using it to throw small rocks at the pair. Then Elsbeth played the video and it showed a couple seconds of it throwing a rock at Dowling.

Ximon was shocked. "Are you telling me they were attacked by some kind of tool-using kangaroos?"

"It looks that way, but I don't think those rocks would have been fatal unless they got really lucky – they'd have hurt, but not likely kill. It certainly caused the team to run off. Now look at this one."

She manipulated the video and showed a clip a few seconds long. In this one, the camera looked up from ground level from Dowling's body (through a bit of blood) and they saw a couple of these creatures huddled around her caressing her and chattering amongst themselves solemnly.

"If I'm not mistaken, this is after they've run from the rocks. Here, Al-Mufti is gone, and Dowling has fallen, perhaps hitting her head as Jaylan said. It likes like these critters are trying to sooth Dowling and it sounds like THEY'RE DISCUSSING IT."

Ximon stared hard at the screen as if it could tell him more "Well, it looks like we know what the 'little things' that Jaylan was referring to are, though this doesn't explain everything. We'll have to look at their external sites for that."

"One more thing, I found a short, broken audio log between the outpost and the shuttle they used to have. It sounds like Lu is leaving in the shuttle they had stowed nearby, and Jaylan is frantically trying to get her to come back or take him. Both are terrified. Listen to Lu's response."

Elsbeth played a short clip from Lu. "Jaylan, I'm sorry, but I'm getting out of here. Those Krichin appear to be tearing our stuff apart, they attacked Dowling, and you've lost it. I KNOW you killed Al-Mufti and you're crazier every day. I'm not sticking around until you decide I'm in league with them and need to be killed. I'm sorry. I'll send help. "

Ximon sent a short message to Iday summarizing all this so he could have it as he talks to Jaylan. Then he and Elsbeth just gathered up what they needed to take until Iday came out a short while later.

Ximon looked at him quizzically, "Well, anything else out of him?"

Iday replied a bit sadly, "Not too much, but he confirmed most of it in a vague sort of way. Based on what you told me and what he said, here's what I think happened…

"These guys were mainly studying those cybexapods but started seeing things that they didn't do, and troublesome stuff started happening around the station. Then Dowling and Al-Mufti were attacked by this little guys and Dowling died, apparently from hitting her head. They were all getting a bit paranoid by then, so it wasn't too much of stretch for Jaylan to believe that Al-Mufti was involved in the killing and Jaylan eventually shot him. Then Jaylan and Lu tried to fix things and call for help for a few days, but Jaylan was getting worse. Eventually Lu left, fearing both Jaylan and what those little things were doing to the outpost. Then Jaylan just sat and stewed until we showed up."

Elsbeth asked "OK, so what do we do now?"

Ximon thought for a moment and looked around the room, considering. "Well, we've got to take him, Mufti's body, and some of this stuff back to the ship, but before we go, we need to go look down that side passage and see if we can find anything else there. I hate to split up, but Elsbeth why don't you stay here while Iday and I go check that side passage out. Then we can figure out the best way to haul everything. Oh, but let me go upstairs here and try to reach Mantis to check in."

Ximon came back a couple minutes later shaking his head and showed them a video. In it, several Krichin approached the air raft and were messing with it. The air raft AI then set off an alarm that scared them off. Then some time later, some of the Krichin came back, broke off the air raft's antenna, and were trying to get in it.

Ximon said, "The air raft AI tried to send us this but couldn't reach us. Mantis was in that link, so she had it capture all this and is having it trigger alarms any time they try to get close. We'd better hurry or we may have air raft problems. Mantis and Raiza were quite worried about us and were relieved we're OK."

So, Ximon and Iday quickly checked out that side passage. It went about a half kilometer to a flat area where the outpost had had their shuttle and air raft stored and then had a shorter path up to where their comm equipment was. The shuttle was, of course, gone but the air raft remained. Or rather, most of an air raft remained. It looked a bit like it had been parked in a bad part of town. Ximon examined it while Iday ran up to where the outpost communication equipment was located.

Ximon noted that the air raft's antennas were gone, as were a whole bunch of instruments, knobs, or other things that would have been easy to break off. A couple storage panels had been pried open so little things like the survival kit, med kit, etc. were taken. They'd also taken a bunch of the loose wiring under the dash.

Iday came back and reported similar for the outpost comms. "I can see where several smaller antennas or dishes were, but they're gone. The bigger dish is still there, but it's not working – some of its components and cabling, as well as some of the power couplers are gone. There is no doubt it was those creatures – there are charred bodies of two of them nearby. I assume they got shocked trying to deal with the power."

Ximon and Iday got back with Elsbeth and gathered stuff up. Besides the three of them, they had to deal with Jaylan and Mufti's body, so they took turns hauling the latter. Jaylan slipped in and out of lucidity and sometimes mourned and carried Mufti like a lost friend. Other times he would weep uncontrollably at seeing Mufti and almost had to be dragged himself. It took a while to get back to the air raft in this way. As they approached, they noticed several of the Krichin observing it from nearby. Most of them scurried off when they got close, but one sat there observing from five meters up a rocky ledge overlooking the area nearby. Ximon motioned the others to the air raft. "Get the stuff stowed. I'm going to try something."

He walked slowly toward the ledge. As Ximon approached, he spoke softly as if the creature could understand. Finally, he looked up at the creature from below and told it they had come in peace and would likely return and hoped to talk to them. The creature then launched into a long bit of chattering that Ximon thought sounded like it could be a solemn speech. Then Ximon solemnly laid down some "gifts" – a headlamp, some food packets, and his hat. He made sure to catch this whole exchange on video and audio.

They got in the air raft and headed back to Mantis. When they got back inside, Raiza greeted them happily but her voice seemed somewhat chiding. "It is good to have you safely back. Mantis and I were most concerned when we lost contact with you and then we saw those creatures near the air raft."

Ximon was almost apologetic. "Well, sorry to keep you in suspense, but I think we're OK."

He had Elsbeth and Iday set up Jaylan in one of the cabins.

As soon as they left, Raiza came up and hugged Ximon. "Ximon, I was very scared for you. Had we not heard from you in a few hours I was considering coming after you."

Ximon hugged her tightly as well. "Now, Raiza. We were OK, but I'll try to be better at watching for lost communication. Now, I'd better get ready for takeoff." So he broke the embrace, kissed her on the forehead, and headed for the bridge.

Iday and Elsbeth joined him a couple minutes later. They had put Jaylan in the room, but first they made sure to take out anything dangerous and Elsbeth jury-rigged the door so he couldn't get out.

As they took off Elsbeth worked with Mantis to relook at the logs from the comm relay. As they were leaving orbit Elsbeth said, "I think I found something," and had Mantis play a short message.

It was a fairly frantic female voice, overlaid with some static. "Jaylan, this is Lu. I hope you're OK. I've been up here for a few days now, but no signs of a ship. I'm going to go out to the gas giant. I should have hope of seeing a ship there. If I find someone, I'll try to come get you. Take care of yourself."

Elsbeth looked at the time stamps on the message. "This was from three days after she left the outpost, but judging by the comms damage we saw, I doubt he ever got it. So he thought he was abandoned and alone, except for little critters tearing up the outpost."

Ximon nodded and pursed his lips. "Good find. Of course, that means we need to take another look at the gas giant before jumping out."

"Yeah, I figured that."

They got out to Cybex Beta 5 and started a moderately fast searching orbit. In a few hours, they detected a shuttle in slow orbit.

Ximon signaled it. "Shuttle, this is the KSS Mantis on an investigation mission to Cybex Beta 3. Please state your mission here."

There was a fast, almost manic, response, "Oh god, Mantis! Thank god you're here. Help me. I'm Humaira Lu from the outpost on Cybex 3. I need help."

"Roger, Lu. We'll dock in a few minutes."

They docked with the shuttle and found Humaira Lu. She wasn't in the best of shape. The shuttle had plenty of power, but Lu had basically no food left, was running short on water, and was taxing the air filtration system. She was also a bit frantic from her experiences and then feeling alone for weeks.
Raiza prepared her a good meal and then they set her up in a room.

Elsbeth asked Ximon, "Why didn't we or that freighter see her before?"

"A gas giant is a big place and we were getting gas, not

searching. Plus, the orbit she was in wasn't where most skimmers would be nor where she could best be seen. Had we got lucky before we might have found her, but no such luck. Also, I'm betting that if we look, her scanners might not be working well."

Elsbeth grinned sardonically. "Well, you know me, I rarely get lucky." Then continued, "I was just about to check out the shuttle. I'll see if that's right about the scanners."

Elsbeth found that, though the shuttle was generally in good shape, a couple of the small sensor antennas were damaged, and Lu hadn't been able to adjust the system to compensate.

"Ximon, it looks like those critters got at the shuttle too before she took off. There wasn't much they could easily get off there, but they tried with those antennas and messed them up in the process."

"Did it look like stuff is working well enough for the shuttle to do an automated landing?"

"Should be if it's an easy one."

Ximon had Mantis coordinate with the shuttle and set the shuttle to land on the smallest of Cybex Beta 5's moons. He also set an auto-response message on it to say, "This is KSF Shuttle Beta 3 Outpost."

He explained, "If anyone finds it, hopefully that'll keep them from stealing it or scavenging it for parts."

Then he announced to the crew, "Prepare for jump. Next stop Moda."

The jump was uneventful. Lu and Jaylan were both relieved to find that the other was OK, though Lu was clearly leery of him. Jaylan was quiet for most of the trip. He was fine most of the time, but had some manic moments, some where he ceaselessly wept, and some where he yelled angrily at being detained. Iday spent a fair amount of time with him, working to calm him down and clarify details of his story.

Ximon, Elsbeth, and Iday worked together to assemble the entire mission report. This included logs audio and video logs, as well as statements from Jaylan and Lu, etc. It also included Ximon's "conversation" with the Krichin watcher. After a couple days, Mantis had been able to decipher that the Krichin were speaking a language and break out a few words from the watcher's speech – peace, sorrow, supplies, sorrow, sorrow ...

The complete report was huge, but the executive summary wasn't too bad.

When they came out of jump in the Moda system, Ximon sent the report to the KSF Station and informed them that the KSS Mantis, would be arriving in approximately 18 hours and that they needed to turn over Jaylan and Lu, the body, and the supplies they were carrying. He also informed them Mantis would be in port for approximately 48 hours thereafter in case they had any questions. This led to a series of radio conversations and Moda Base was ready to receive them.

As they approached the station at Moda 3, Ximon gathered everyone in the galley. "We'll be docking at Moda Scout Station in 30 minutes. We'll be met by the station commander. Jaylan/Lu, we'll turn you and Al-Mufti over to them. I'm sure they'll have questions for you and will probably want to do a medical work up. Crew, we'll plan to be at Moda for approximately 72 hours. They may want to interview each of us. So, you can have a couple day shore leave, but you need to stay in contact" with this he looked meaningfully at Elsbeth "... so they can get with us if they need to."

Elsbeth just rolled her eyes at that.

"In any case, we'll probably need an hour or two before we can run off. And I'd like everyone to send me a message with their general plan and check in two hours before our planned launch time. I'll update you if the launch time changes."

Elsbeth nodded and looked at her tablet. "I've sent you a list of a few things I'd like to buy while we're here if I can find them."

They landed at the designated bay and shut Mantis down. Ximon, Elsbeth, Iday, and Raiza accompanied by Jaylan and Lu, headed down the ramp.

As they came down the ramp, a group of eight Scout personnel came up, including a gurney, a forklift, and a wheeled cart.

The leader wearing a KSF dress coat shook everyone's hand, "Welcome, I'm Commander Codoc, welcome to Moda Station. We're anxious to help these folks and the additional detail related to the outpost. Your report already went out by Comm Boat."

Then he pointed to folks as he detailed them. "Dr. Jacobs and her folks would like to take Specialist Lu back for a medical exam as well as claim the remains of Al-Mufti. Sergeants Lombard and Heyns here will take Specialist Zaitsev in for some questioning and medical evaluation. Our logistics crew will get that cargo. And I'd like to briefly chat with you."

"Of course, sir. Iday, if you'd hand off Jaylan there to Security; Elsbeth, please help the logistics crew get the cargo out and hand over the physical artifacts from the outpost; and Raiza, please take the Dr and her team to Al-Mufti's body. Everyone, please get digital receipts."

Everyone then scattered, leaving Ximon and CDR Codec. Codec had Ximon give him a brief summary of the overall mission, a general assessment of Lu and Zaitsev, and his thoughts on the Krichin and dealing with them. Ximon generally repeated what he had in the report but made sure to applaud Lu and to stress Zaitsev's mental state. As far as the Krichin, he suggested a specialized translate, contact, and trade team be sent out.

Ximon concluded, "I don't think they intentionally killed Dowling nor recognized that they were doing harm in the stuff they took. I think they're aggressive scavengers who got scared when Mufti and Dowling came near their home. Consider them like any relatively primitive race, but they clearly had an interest in metal and technological things. What will happen to Lu and Zaitsev?"

Codec's brow knit in thought as he considered that for a moment before he answered. "Hard to be sure with the 'wheels of justice' and all that. But Lu will probably go through some medical and psych eval. If she's fine, she'll probably be given some extra pay, a few weeks off, and a new posting. Zaitsev too will get some medical eval, but heavy on the psych. Then, we'll probably try him, though whether the outcome is a penal colony or a mental institution (or both) is hard to say."

Then he added, "Good work here Sabo, you cleared up a mystery, saved two of four scouts, got us info on a potential contact, and put the shuttle where we can have it picked up. If you choose to file your invoice while here, I'll try to expedite it. I've got your info from the report, but I'll probably need each of you to come in the security folks briefly and give a legal statement re Zaitsev. I'll have them arrange something with each of you. I think I have what I need, but I'll contact you and take you to lunch if I need more."

"Thanks, commander. Happy to help."

By that time, the doc's team had claimed the body and left with Lu in a wheelchair (despite her protests), the Security folks had taken Jaylan in for questioning, and the logistics team was making good headway on the cargo.

Ximon sent a message to the crew, "I show 1740. Unless we must change it, launch time will be 1800 in three days. Please send me your general plans and plan for a formal interview with Security. Have fun .... But not TOO much fun."

Then he told Iday, "You can head out whenever you like.

If you don't stay here, I'll see you in a few days."

Iday nodded. "I already have an interview scheduled with Security. I may be here intermittently but need to spend some time at my church."

"Very well, Godspeed, I guess."

Iday smiled at that and went in to get his bag.

Ximon went over and told Elsbeth, "You're free to go as soon as we 'button her up.' I approved that parts request. You'll hear from Security if you haven't. If I don't see you, have fun."

Elsbeth laughed in reply, "You know me – I'm the master of fun. But I'll be here at least some, fixing a few things."

Ximon nodded, went in the ship, and found Raiza. He told her, "Raiza, I know you don't need it, but I'd like you to accompany me out to dinner and for a little shopping. Let's leave in 20 minutes. Please wear something nice."

"Ximon, that sounds wonderful. I'll look forward to it and wear something appropriate that you like."

Ximon then took a quick shower and put on some decent clothes. Raiza was awaiting him in the galley in 15 minutes, with her hair done nicely and wearing a short black dress, stockings, and stiletto heels.

"You look lovely, Raiza."

"As do you Ximon. Thank you."

Then he took her arm and they headed for town – the shops about a half kilometer away. Ximon enjoyed having a dazzlingly beautiful women, dressed 'to the nines' on his arm, even if she was a robot. They found a restaurant that sounded good to Ximon and had a nice dinner. Raiza primarily made conversation but 'ate' a little bit of Ximon's meal. Raiza didn't digest anything, but studies had shown that having companion bots participate in the act of eating made others, such as Ximon, more comfortable.

They hit a few clothing stores and Ximon had Raiza try on several outfits and bought her some, including some lingerie. Then they just walked the main drag, quietly enjoying one another's company. Ximon reflected that she was, indeed, good company.

Except for a Security interview the next day, the time in port was quite relaxing. He took Raiza out a few times and they saw a few Vids and nearby sites.

Elsbeth was in and out, fixed a few things, and was never visibly drunk when Ximon saw her. Ximon only saw Iday briefly a couple days later. He was clearly busy with 'his work.'

Ximon filed his invoice for the mission and was again excited to be paid well and quickly. Again, he got more than the mission specifically offered for rescue, legal assistance, and for salvaging the shuttle. He also looked at other jobs, but didn't sign up for any.

He was set up and ready to go a few hours before the planned launch time and messaged the team. "Raiza will have a dinner ready one hour before launch time if you choose to join us."

Elsbeth replied, "I'll be there approximately 30 minutes before launch. Don't eat everything."

Iday showed up a couple hours early, ate and was ready go.

They took off without incident and were on their way to jump. Since they had official business at the Scout Station, the KSF had fueled up Mantis so they didn't need to skim. They reached the jump point and jumped without incident, or so it seemed ..."

JAUNT 3: MIS-JUMP

They spent the jump in relaxation and/or boredom. Ximon took some refresher classes on navigation procedures, spent time with Raiza, and generally checked on Mantis. Among other things, he taught Raiza some more rudiments of shooting. She'd never be a good shot because her brain just wasn't engineered for that, but she could hold the gun properly, discharge shots consistently at a nearby target, and reload. You never knew when that might come in handy.

The rest of the crew got along well. There were no arguments and Elsbeth was never too visibly drunk and didn't complain of nightmares. Iday was his quiet, studious self.

... and then all hell broke loose.

Mantis came out of jump suddenly and with a jarring lurch almost two hours earlier than planned. Ximon was knocked off his feet at the sudden and unexpected change in momentum. He got up yelling as he sprinted to the bridge. "Mantis, what the hell? Iday, to the bridge and PRAY! Elsbeth, what the holy hell?"

As he ran, Mantis said, "Captain, I'm checking our stellar position, but initial indications suggest that we have not exited jump at the intended destination. There are no immediate navigational dangers."

Ximon dove into his seat and started scanning the area.

Ximon yelled at Iday as he sat down, "Navigational Fixes, now!"

They were relatively clear space, with a planet at about 15 million kilometers and a Red Dwarf star at 150 million kilometers. So they were a fair ways out in whatever system they were in.

Ximon started longer range scans. "OK, Iday, where are we?"

Iday somewhat sheepishly said, "Well we're definitely NOT in the intended system, I'm still working on the final fix."

"Mantis, what do you show?"

Mantis said, "I concur that we're not in the Chater system. My two-star fix indicates a 95% probability of the Cruna Sigma system. Verifying three-star fix now."

Iday interjected, relieved to have caught up, "I'm showing Cruna so far as well. Still working."

Ximon took a deep breath and closed his eyes for a second. "Elsbeth, what's going on down there?"

"Ximon, I'm checking. I'll let you know when I find something."

Mantis then said, "Captain, my three-star fix confirms Cruna Sigma with 98% probability."

Iday just nodded in confirmation.

Ximon looked exasperated and worried. "OK, then Mantis, tell us about the Cruna Sigma system."

Mantis read off the details. "The Cruna Sigma System is 48.7 light years from the intended Chater system and approximately 30.6 light years coreward of Tixaya. Cruna Sigma is a Red Dwarf star. The system contains four planets and eight dwarf planets. It contains no known permanent human settlements."

Ximon, "… and the planets? How bad are we screwed?"

Mantis said, "Captain, I do not understand the reference to screwed. Does this refer to sexual activity or mechanical construction?"

"Just tell me about the planets."

Mantis reported, "Sigma 1 is a dense planet. 0.2 AU, 4500 km diameter, no moons frequently afflicted by flares in the solar corona. Sigma 2 is larger, rocky planet with an iron core and a trace atmosphere, 0.4 AU, 9000 kilometers diameter, two moons. Sigma 3 is larger planet, rocky core, and a moderately dense, toxic atmosphere, 0.9A AU, 11000 km diameter, 1 moon. Sigma 4 is a pseudo-gas giant planet, 5.0 AU, 39,000 kilometer diameter, nine moons. Would you like to hear about the dwarf planets as well?"

"No thanks."

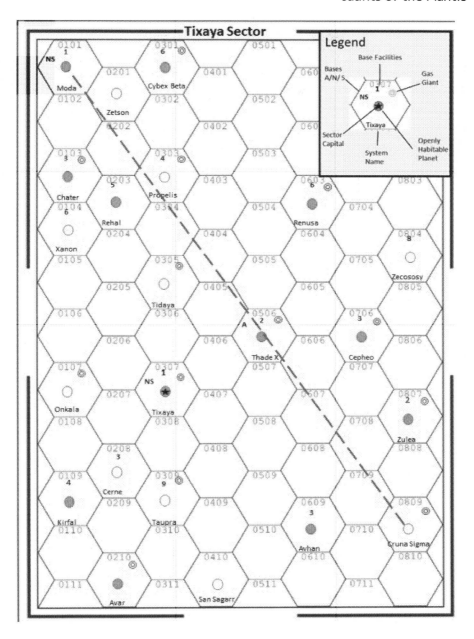

Ximon pointed to the navigational screen, "So what are we looking at?"

Iday indicated their location on the screen. "We're approximately one AU from the star, between Sigma 3 and 4. Approximately 15 million kilometers from Sigma 3 and 600 million kilometers from Sigma 4.

Mantis added, "With our jump range, we can get to the Zulea system, which is on a jump ten range route to Tixaya and has a permanent station."

Ximon considered all this. "While our play would be to try to skim at Sigma 4, we're going to go do a quick survey of Sigma 3. We're now officially looking for paying work and KSF might pay us for that."

Ximon said, "Iday, take us to Sigma 3 and into orbit" then he headed to Engineering. En route he told Mantis, "Alert me of any nav or piloting issues."

In Engineering Elsbeth was running back and forth between a console and an open magnetic coil array. She saw Ximon, scowled, and kept moving. "I'm still not sure Ximon. Stay out of the way."

Ximon sat calmly down and watched.

In a couple minutes, as she ran back and forth, Elsbeth said in exasperation, "It looks like we had a failure in one of the field alignment coils, but I'm trying to verify, figure out which one, AND why the heck it happened. The fields have been very stable until now. I'll let you know when I know."

Ximon just sat quietly for ten minutes or so. He was just letting her cool down and answer in her own time.

Elsbeth added, "Yes, definitely a failure in field alignment coil. Looks like number four, but I'm testing all of them. Really, Ximon, this could take hours until I can give you a definitive answer."

"Ok, just one question. The maneuvering engines show fine on the boards. Is there any reason we can't use them?

"Damn, I hope not. It may be days before we can jump."

"Good, I was a bit afraid of that delay."

"It won't do us a bit of good to try to jump soon, mis-jump again, and break the jump drive in the process. Don't even think about jumping until I tell you."

"I wouldn't dream of it. Good luck."

He left Engineering and headed to his room. On the way, he told Iday, "Give her 0.8G, what's our ETA to Sigma 3?"

Iday replied in a few seconds, "Roger, ETA about five hours."

"Roger. Hold her steady and alert me if you see anything on scans."

When he passed through the galley, he grabbed Razia's hand and led her to their room. He definitely needed some quick stress relief.

In 45 minutes, he was back on the bridge and swapped seats with Iday.

"So, Iday, like I said we're doing these scans in hopes we earn something from it. Aside from that, it gives Elsbeth a little more time to check everything and, if need be, fix something. As you probably know, if you mis-jump, you don't want to be too quick to jump again or the problem could get worse."

Iday nodded sagely. "Certainly. Prudence is dictated."

As they approached Sigma 3, Elsbeth reported, "Ximon, I finished testing the coils. It's just coil four. It's not something I can fix here. When we get to a station I can test more thoroughly, but there's a good chance it will have to be replaced."

Ximon groaned. "Well, crap, that sounds expensive. Can we jump again and, if so, when do you think?"

"Well, I know it's at least 14 hours or so until we get out to Sigma 4, so probably around then. Like I said, I can't fix the coil, but I can adjust the field so that it should compensate fairly well. I may send y'all some tweaked parameters for when you're planning your jump. I'll let you know on that."

"Roger, Elsbeth. Keep up the good work. Would an extra set of hands help?"

"Not any of yours, at least not now. But I might in a few hours."

They got to Sigma 3 and entered the atmosphere. Ximon said, "OK, Iday, I'm going to make a total of five orbital passes. Conduct a full range of planetary scans and let me know if you see anything interesting and need another pass to verify."

"Yes, Ximon."

About that time arrived with some sandwiches, snacks, drinks. Ximon had asked her to bring some up and take some to Elsbeth.

Ximon said, "Thank you Raiza. This helps."

"My pleasure, Captain. Let me know if you need anything else."

The scans of the planet were uneventful and neither Iday nor Mantis noted anything substantially different, so they broke orbit and headed for Cruna Sigma 4. Ximon and Iday then took turns flying, swapping every 3 hours.

Cruna Sigma 4:
>*Diameter: 39,000 km*
>*Distance from sun: 5.0 AU*
>*Atmosphere: Gas Giant, Moderate Density. Hydrogen, Helium, and numerous trace elements*

Gravity: 1.5 G
Temperature Range: -250 - -150 C
Magnetic Field: Moderate
Lifeforms: None detected

When they were about four hours out, Ximon again ventured to Engineering. Elsbeth was buttoning up the mag field coil access panel. "Well, your timing is good this time. I've adjusted the coils to compensate for number four. It should produce a solid, stable field. My eyes are bleary so I'm going to take a break for an hour or so and then double check a few things."

"OK, sounds good."

In a couple hours, Elsbeth sent them some revised parameters to use in their jump calculations and Ximon and Iday redid the jump solution to compensate. Ximon made sure that he, Iday, and Mantis all used them in calculations.

Ximon was flying as they approached Sigma 4. As Ximon was doing a deceleration burn, an alert light came on and Iday said, "I just detected a vessel near that nearest moon – it just came from behind the moon."

Ximon said, "Scan it – we need data." Then to the ship, "Strap in now, we have to burn."

Then he hailed the ship, "UI Vessel this is the KSS Mantis on a survey mission. Please identify yourself and state your business."

A gruff voice on the other ship replied, "Mantis you are intruding in our space. Prepare to be boarded."

Ximon was deeply concerned. "That doesn't sound good. What do we have?"

Iday read from his screens. "It's about 500 tons, medium freighter class. It's burning toward us."

Mantis added, "It's on a direct intercept course, is burning at almost 2G, and is actively scanning us. It is showing no transponder, in direction violation of the law."

The other ship hailed again. "Continue deceleration and prepare to be boarded or we WILL fire. You're not on a mission here."

Ximon radioed back, "You are interfering with an official Republic mission" and cut off.

In the bridge he said, "We're flying. We can continue this discussion at a distance."

Ximon then fired maneuvering jets to flip the ship 150 degrees to port as the other ship was coming from about 30-degree starboard. The maneuver imposed almost 3Gs and had them all grunting, but it got them facing away from the other vessel. Mantis hadn't fully decelerated, so it still had substantial momentum. Ximon then fired thrusters, burning at 2.5G. This pushed them into their seats and caused major stomach lurches because of the repeated changes of forces.

As they were turning, the other ship started firing. It launched two missiles at them and then fired a light laser cannon. The laser missed badly because they definitely weren't planning on the maneuver Mantis pulled, but the missiles kept coming.

Ximon yelled, "Iday, get firing that chaff thrower!" and then he dove for the outer atmosphere of the giant. He announced, "This is going to get rough – we're under fire!"

Elsbeth screamed angrily in response. "Going to GET rough!?!? That jackassery about killed me down here."

Iday started firing the chaff thrower. The whole intent of the chaff thrower was to put clouds of 'chaff' in the sky between you and whoever's shooting at you. If there was a significant enough cloud between you and the shooter, it would diffract, deflect, or absorb a portion of the power of any lasers passing through it, either making them miss or reducing how much damage they did. However, since everyone was moving so fast, to be effective, you had to be pretty good at guessing relative positions.

Mantis was pulling away from the UI ship, but not the missiles, and the ship's laser kept firing. The chaff thrower worked well on one shot that could really have damaged them. It diffracted or absorbed so much energy that what hit them did no real damage.

Ximon said, "Mantis, can you tell me about those missiles?"

"They appear to be homing, likely standard configuration. They could cripple us if they hit."

"Mantis, hit them with all sensors at full power. See if you can blind or confuse them."

Mantis was just entering the atmosphere with the missiles gaining. Ximon kept diving deeper into the atmosphere, dodging and diving in the process. He said, "Everyone, prepare for severe turbulence, Gs, and possible impact."

"Let's see if they like the atmosphere as much as we do."

Mantis said, "Captain, our angle of attack relative to the atmosphere is out of recommend limits, we're encountering serious turbulence and hull temperature is rising precipitously."

"Roger, Mantis, but we have other problems right now. Keep shooting that chaff thrower."

The combat display showed the missiles getting ever nearer, but the other ship seemed to have stopped shooting their laser – what the sand wasn't impacting, the atmosphere was.

As the missiles were 100 kilometers or less out, one of them veered off course toward a hot bubble of gas in the atmosphere, but the other kept coming.

The other missile ticked closer as the Mantis bucked wildly in the atmosphere, but as it got within 10 kilometers the missile was bucked by harsh turbulence repeatedly and started tumbling. It soon started falling behind and then exploded. The combat display showed them all clear except the freighter falling back. It appeared to have dropped its thrust. Soon it disappeared, though this was likely due to atmospheric interference rather than distance.

Ximon breathed for the first time in several minutes, reduced their thrust considerably, and stopped descending into the atmosphere. "Ok crew, we literally dodged a bullet, but we've still got baddies out there."

Iday didn't look up from his screen. "We can outrun them, but we'll need to pull out of the atmosphere to do so safely."

"Roger, just trying to put a bit more distance before we do." Then he turned about 20 degrees more starboard.

They continued on in grave silence for a few more minutes, then Ximon slowly nudged up out of the atmosphere just as Mantis said, "Captain, I must urge you to slow down or leave the atmosphere. We will soon sustain damage if you maintain this course of action."

As they pulled out of the thicker bands of atmosphere, the UI vessel re-appeared on the combat display, but it was a lot farther back. It apparently saw them too.

Iday announced, "They just put two more birds in the air inbound."

"This time we run." He was confident that they had enough range and velocity that they could outrun them. Still, he fired a 3G burn, slamming them all back in their seats, and pulled farther up out of the atmosphere to avoid drag. The missiles started gaining, but only very slowly, and the UI vessel kept falling farther back.

They continued like this for about 15 minutes when the missiles apparently ran out of fuel and started fading behind them.

Ximon said, "OK, we got lucky again. Now, I'm going to try to put a planet between us and this guy." So, they continued accelerating around the planet.

"Mantis, how long will it take us to skim for sufficient fuel to make the calculated jump?"

"Captain, it will take about 50 minutes at the safest recommended skimming speed of..."

Ximon cut her off, "Roger. We're going to burn like this for about 90 minutes and then we're going to do a burn to slow and sink down in the atmosphere to start skimming."

Elsbeth spoke up, "Don't you dare deploy that scoop above max skimming speed! It won't take the strain and if we lose that, it's game over."

"Got ya. I'm not THAT crazy."

Then Ximon quietly radioed Raiza, "How are you doing girl?"

"Ximon, I am relieved the ship was not damaged. I am safely strapped in in the galley but was slightly damaged by some items that were not secured when you executed high G maneuvers. However, it is minor and does not affect my operations. Is there anything I can do to assist you?"

"No, nothing at this time. I'm sorry you're hurt. I'll help you fix that as soon as we're safe. Are you sure you won't sustain more damage from the wound?"

"Ximon, thank you, but no. I am not leaking any system fluids and believe I have secured most potential debris. I apologize – I failed to detect the unsecured items and secure them promptly."

Ximon whispered, "I'll spank you later. Be careful" and broke the connection.

She messaged his comm a few seconds later, "I will happily bare the appropriate portions of my anatomy at an appropriate time." This was followed by a wink emoji.

Ximon smiled at that and refocused.

They were putting a lot of sky between them and the UI vessel and it soon dropped behind the horizon.

Ximon said, "Iday, what would you do if you were in his position?"

Iday thought for a moment. "We are faster but can't shoot back and have to skim to truly escape. I think his most logical course is to continue to build up speed in hopes of catching us when we try to skim. He can stay high and keep thrust on while we must stop thrust AND deal with heavy atmospheric drag. We can get enough planet between us that it would take him a while to get close enough, but a lot will depend on how well he can predict where we are. By the time we're done skimming, he'll have a lot more momentum"

"Understood, I'm hoping to confuse him a bit."

"I hope it works."

After about an hour more of burn, Ximon said, "Ok, kids, now we decelerate, dive, and skim. Prepare for Gs."

There were, in fact, a lot Gs. Ximon flipped the ship 180, burned at about 3G to decelerate quickly. As Mantis bled velocity badly, Ximon stared turning more to port until their vector about 90 degrees off their past course. He also started descending, using the atmosphere to slow them more, though the turbulence was substantial. As soon as it was safe to do so, Ximon pushed Mantis into the thicker atmosphere, slowing her further.

Mantis protested, "Again, captain, this velocity in atmosphere risks damage to the hull and external components."

"Noted Mantis, but you'll thank me if we survive this."

"I will thank you if that is the case and if you so direct. However, I would definitely appreciate being intact at that point."

As they continued to slow, the turbulence reduced and Ximon went deeper and kept turning. Then Ximon said, "Deploying scoop and commencing skimming. We're below threshold velocity."

Mantis said, "But captain, we're skimming considerably deeper in the atmosphere than is recommended."

"Roger, Mantis. Elsbeth, keep an eye on the skimming system."

"Sure, Ximon, I'll let you know if our hull falls off."

"Mantis/Iday, passive scanners only, but watch for that guy to reappear."

As they skimmed, Ximon kept diving, turning, and slowing. Eventually, their course was almost 90 degrees off the vector they'd had when running from the UI ship.

After about 20 minutes Mantis noted, "I'm detecting the other ship's active scans, but they're behind us and off our course. That, coupled with the density of the atmosphere makes it unlikely they can detect us."

Ximon almost whispered, "Mantis turn off anything that would emanate significantly." Then he jokingly added, "Crew, rig for silent running."

They continued skimming slowly and deeply, and were all quiet, afraid that the other ship could somehow hear them.

"Mantis, what's our jump fuel percentage?"

"We're at approximately 50% of the minimum necessary for the calculated jump."

They continued for 20, then 30, minutes, hearing and seeing nothing of the other ship. Mantis read off the fuel percentage every few minutes. Ximon waited until they had substantially more than jump minimum.

Finally, Ximon retracted the scoop and told Iday, "Pray for us and watch those displays."

Ximon then started a low thrust and started pulling VERY slowly up out of the atmosphere.

Ximon ordered Mantis, "Mantis, project his position if he maintains his current course and velocity."

"Roger, Captain, it's plotted on the main screen and will be continually updated, but it's only a projection based on assumption of his behavior. As you know, human behavior is difficult to project with a strong baseline of historical decision making by that individual. Even then, individual actions can vary widely from that baseline of behavior."

The projection showed the other ship proceeding swiftly around the planet, ever farther from them.

Ximon touched the screen. "... and now add our plot at this velocity."

It showed the Mantis relatively creeping in the other direction.

Mantis continued slowly gaining speed and altitude with still no sign of the other ship. Finally, by the time they were fully out of the heavy bands of the atmosphere, they had picked up some speed.

Ximon turned to Iday. "Anything on long range sensors?"

Iday shook his head. "Nothing, but I'm seeing echoes of his pings – looks like they're past the horizon."

Now Ximon applied a full 3G thrust, again sinking the entire crew into their seats.

"Mantis, show me a projection of the paths and velocities of the moons in our arc."

Mantis quickly threw up a display with the moons that are in this arc of the planet in view.

Ximon breathed a sigh of relief. "OK, now we're going to try to increase our odds by going past Moon 1 up there."

Ximon flew so they'd be crossing just behind the moon's orbital path. Since the moon was currently orbiting faster than the Mantis was running and had its own substantial gravity, Mantis could get a "gravity boost" to its acceleration and a slight course change to one flatter relative to the orbits of the moons.

Ximon ordered, "Iday, get some imagery and short-range scans of these moons as we go by, but stay ready on the Chaff Thrower. Mantis, watch long-range scan for ships or enemy sensor activity."

Moon 1 loomed large as they approached. It was large, a sickly mottled yellow-green color, and a very rough surface.

As they neared the moon and got farther from the planet Mantis noted, "Moon One's gravity can now be detected as its own substantive source."

As they got ever nearer Iday said, "The moon has a faint atmosphere, a very mountainous surface, and appears to be volcanically active. Once we go past her, that'll give a little more 'haze' to make us harder to find."

Ximon said, "OK, this is our nearest approach, now we continue burning as she pulls along past her."

They continued burning with the moon as a large presence on the screen, with the much larger planet behind. Soon they whipped past, gaining velocity from the moon's pull, and started pulling away from the moon (getting farther from the planet as the moon stayed at its constant orbital distance).

"Mantis, give me a calculation." Then he tapped two of the farther out moons in arc and said, "Could we get a gravity boost from either of these two?"

"Captain, moon 4 is too far out of synch with our path and relative speeds. Moon 7 will work. I've displayed the optimal path."

"OK, matching that path. Iday, watch for sensor echoes."

They sped on in that direction, continuing to burn hard. This moon was more of a typical mottled grey rock.

As it loomed close, Iday fairly shouted, "The ship has crossed the horizon. It's turned about and is coming our way and it's got two shuttles deployed. The ship has greater velocity than us and continues to burn hard. They've got every sensor blazing."

"Ok, let me know if they hit us with active sensors. Mantis, do imagery and scans as we go past the moon."

Just before they passed behind the moon, Iday said, "We were just hit in an active sensor sweep."

"We'll see if that lasts."

Then they were crossing on the far side of the moon and being pulled by its gravity. They got another good velocity boost as they pulled away.

"Mantis, plot our velocities again. Can they catch us?"

A new plot of the velocities appeared, it showed them speeding ever farther from the planet with the ship and two shuttles pounding after. They didn't intersect within the field shown.

"Captain, assuming we continue burning at this rate and that the thrust we've seen from the ship so far is its maximum, it cannot catch us. However, the shuttles are an unknown variable. One or both might have higher thrust than they've demonstrated. If so, they might catch us."

"What about missiles?"

"Missiles fired at this range would not catch us. They would make relative progress against our velocity but would likely run out of thrust and then could not catch up."

An alarm chimed and Iday fiddled with knobs on his controls. "They're testing that. The ship just launched two missiles and one of the shuttles just increased its burn."

"Elsbeth, if you can kick the maneuver drive and give us any more thrust that'd be great."

Elsbeth said shortly, "There's not much more it can give. If we try, it could damage her."

They sped on, receding from the planet and pulling away from the enemy ship and its shuttle number one, but with missiles blazing rapidly toward them and the shuttle number two making headway against them.

The missiles continued their acceleration for about 15 minutes and started to get worrisome.

Iday said, "Captain, those must be extra long-range missiles. They're still closing. Intercept in 10 minutes if they continue."

But shortly thereafter, the missiles did run out of gas and could thrust no more. Since Mantis continued to thrust, it pulled away and the missiles just continued an impotent flight behind them.

Iday then said, "That shuttle is still gaining ground, but it has a long way to go. I'm scanning it."

After a few minutes he said, "It looks like a 30-ton ship's boat. It's hitting us with active sensors, so there's a good bet it's got some kind of weapons."

"I wouldn't expect it would be following us without its buddies if it didn't. Keep that chaff thrower ready."

"It's turned into a direct stern chase – he's directly after of us and burning hard to catch us. If he's got lasers, he could be in range within two minutes."

"OK, keep chaff between him and us."

"Firing now" and Iday started firing the chaff thrower periodically.

Alarms then flared and Mantis said, "We have been hit by a beam laser. I see very minor hull damage. However, repeated hits or chance hits could damage key components or the engines."

Iday said, "He's firing at extreme range, but he's getting closer."

Ximon said, "Elsbeth, any issues back there?"

"No, but if we take a hit on the engines, they'll likely crap out or start sputtering."

"Roger. Hey, do we have any loose crates in the cargo bay?"

Elsbeth was silent for a moment. "Sure, we've got a few empties. But what you're thinking won't work; they'd just burn up in our plume."

"Not if there ain't no plume."

"Ximon this is a real bad idea."

"Noted but get on that arm and get the crates in position. Tell me when you're ready."

Iday, interjected, "They are almost exactly aft of us and they're certainly making no effort to evade."

The enemy shuttle fired a few more times over the next few minutes, but most of it was diffracted by chaff and Mantis took no real damage.

After a couple minutes, Elsbeth said, "It's ready, but I still say this is a bad idea."

"Great, now everyone, get ready. Elsbeth, open the rear

cargo hatch. Right after they fire next, I'll say, 'go.' Then, I'll cut our burn. Iday, you'll fire more chaff as a distraction, and Elsbeth, you'll turn off the mags holding the crates down and nudge them with the arm if you have to. Be ready!"

Alerts came on as Mantis registered the rear cargo catch opened.

A few seconds later Iday said, "They've fired again and missed."

Ximon yelled, "Cutting burn. Go, go, go!"

Iday fired several shots of chap as fast as he could. The "chaff" went out in canisters and it didn't explode and spread right away, so it was a few seconds before the chaff canisters opened. In that time, sensors noted two crates away and a few seconds later a large one and a smaller one away. All tumbled as they floated behind the ship.

Elsbeth said, "Closing hatch."

They then waited a few tense seconds.

Mantis noted, "Shuttle is attempting to maneuver to avoid crates but is intercepting the containers too fast. In three, two, one!"

Iday looked excitedly at his screen. "I see it, the shuttle hit at least one large crate."

Ximon then hit full burn again and started evading, juking and jiving up, down, left, and right, "Let's see what effect that had."

Iday said, "I can't tell anything on scanners, but I'm not seeing their active scanners on line."

They flew on for tense seconds. The shuttle fired again but missed entirely. It tried again several more times but continued to miss.

After few minutes of feeble attempts, the shuttle cut its thrust and soon started receding behind them with the rest of the bad guys.

Mantis, "The shuttle has cut its thrust and appears to be maneuvering slightly, about 20 degrees off an intercept course …"

As they watched over the next 30 minutes or so, the ship and its shuttles, now way in the distance, backed up and turned away.

Ximon said, "Continuing 3G until we increase the range. Good work everyone. Catch your breath. 5 hours to jump point."

Ximon cut the thrust after about 45 minutes with no signs of the UI ship pursuing.

"Iday, you have the con, keep her steady to the jump point. Mantis, alert me if you see them come this way on long-range sensors."

"Roger, Captain."

Then Ximon announced, "You can unbuckle if you need to get around, pick up your area, stretch your legs, or hit the head. But be ready in case we need to burn again."

Ximon went back to the galley and found Raiza headed for their room.

"Raiza, how are you? Let me help you."

"Thank you Ximon. I am fully functional but need to re-pair this tear in my skin covering."

They got to their room and Ximon helped her unclothe to reveal a nasty tear in the skin along the front of her left leg. Ximon examined it closely. It didn't appear that any actuators, sensors, or pneumatics were damaged. Had she been human, she would have lost a lot of blood and there would have been a chance of a bleed out from a nick to the femoral artery.

Ximon applied the special resin and skin graft/patch kit

to repair the tear, tenderly spreading the gel and smoothing the edges.

"I'm so glad you're ok." He hugged her tightly, avoiding the repair, for a few minutes while the patch dried completely. "How's that?"

"I appreciate your help and your comfort Ximon. You have healed me. I am yours."

"Oh, you cheeky minx," and pinched her buttock. "Let's wait a bit for that. Why don't you get on some untorn clothes, make sure there's nothing else loose in the galley, and then join us on the bridge."

"Happily, Ximon. I believe that the crew would benefit from some food and beverages as well. I will provide some before I join you on the bridge."

After a pit stop Ximon was back on the bridge and relieved Iday. Raiza arrived about five minutes later and gave him his favorite sandwich and drink and kissed him on the cheek. Then she strapped into the sensor operator seat.

Ximon radioed Elsbeth, "Elsbeth, how's everything looking back there?"

She said snarkily, "Well, you don't appear to have destroyed anything, despite your best efforts. Everything looks good to jump. As soon as we do, I'm taking a long, hot shower, and a long nap – I got banged up pretty good."

"Do you need medical assistance?"

"No, you can keep the 'nurse' to yourself. I'm mainly just sore."

After a little while Ximon announced, "Jumping to the Zulea system in five minutes."

Then, they jumped, and everything seemed to go OK. They were in the silence of jump.

"Again, good work everyone. Take a good long break."

"Mantis, alert me of any issues. I'll be in my room."

He took Raiza by the hand and led her toward their room, whispering in her ear, "Now about that spanking ..." and swatted her butt playfully.

She replied in a sultry voice, "Yes, Ximon, I've been a very bad girl."

The entire jump was quiet. Ximon rested, studied, and fretted over whether this jump would be OK. Iday did his quiet study in his room and occasionally made some meals for everyone. Some items he made were a bit too hot for Elsbeth's tastes, but Ximon enjoyed most of it. Elsbeth fixed up some stuff that had been impacted in the frantic battle and kept fine tuning things. Raiza kept them all well fed and Ximon happy. In addition to other pastimes, Raiza was fairly skilled at several board or computer games that Ximon enjoyed. A couple times they got Elsbeth and/or Iday to join them and all seemed to enjoy it.

Finally, on day six Mantis noted, "Captain, assuming all worked as intended, we should exit jump to the Zulea system in eight hours."

JAUNT 4: ZULEA

Ximon was tracking the jump exit but appreciated the reminder. He ate and got to the bridge four hours early, just in case. Then he sat and waited. Nothing odd happened, and they came out of jump as planned. By that time both Iday and Elsbeth had joined him on the bridge and Raiza was using the handholds at the back of the bridge.

The stars reappeared and their inertia returned as normal.

"Mantis, do a 360 scan for any obstacles or vessels. Iday, get a position check. Elsbeth, run through the systems panel." Ximon then scanned around visually and with sensors behind them. It looked all clear.

Mantis answered first, "No obstacles or vessels are noted within 10,000 km. There are some meteors at 30,000 kilometers, but they are not on an intercept course. Nearest planet is 2.1 million kilometers sunward."

Iday added, "Two stars, Zulea. Checking three stars." He was getting better at this.

Mantis added, "Confirmed Zulea with two stars."

Then Elsbeth, "I'm seeing green across the board."

Ximon breathed a sigh of relief. "Glad to be where we're supposed to be. Thanks everyone and, Iday, thank that god of yours."

"I always do."

Mantis continued, "The planet 2.1 million kilometers sunward is Zulea Decats. It is 4.1 billion kilometers to the station at Zulea Prima, the third planet. There is a dwarf planet,

Zulea Sub 1, 0.3 million kilometers sunward."

Ximon turned to Elsbeth. "Oh crap, we're outside some of the dwarfs. Let me guess, all those adjustment parameters you gave us for the jump were safety factors, causing us to wind up as far from the sun as humanly possible."

"What did you expect, we'd just misjumped, we've got a bad coil, and I had to work to compensate to even make a jump remotely safe. Would you rather adjust to closer to the sun … LIKE IN IT!?!?"

Mantis then interjected, "Captain, I'm detecting a vessel at 150,000 kilometers anti-sunward."

Ximon had to think about that one. "What's anyone but us doing way out here? Iday, scan it. Mantis, plot it's vector."

Ximon hailed it. "UI Vessel, this is KSS Survey Craft Mantis on a survey mission. Please ID and state your purpose."

Raiza said, "Captain, are we technically on a survey mission at this time?"

Tixaya Sector

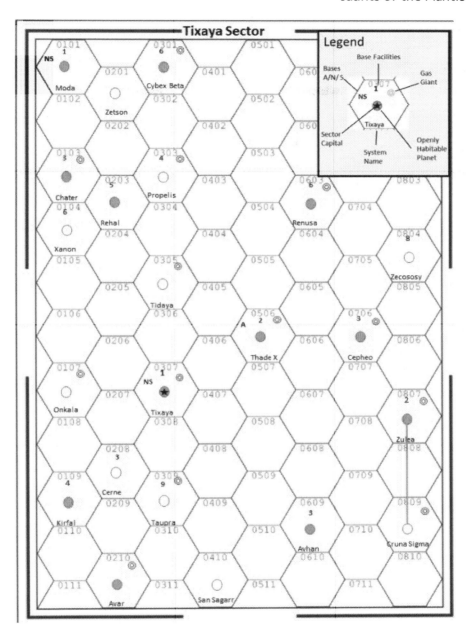

"Perhaps not technically, we're on a pay-our-way-home mission. However, we're scouts so we're kind of always on a survey mission."

"Understood, Captain. Thank you for the clarification."

Mantis said, "Captain, I have plotted its vector. Its slow path is almost directly perpendicular to the sunward path."

Ximon stroked his chin. "Interesting." Then more to himself, "What's he up to? Hopping from one dwarf to another?"

Iday said, "I don't believe he's up to anything. I'm detecting virtually no power readings, no transponder, and no scanners, active or passive. She might be dead. She's appears to be a 400-ton medium freighter."

"Interesting. Let's check it out. Mantis, give me an intercept course."

Mantis plotted a course to take them to within 1km of the vessel.

"Captain, the plotted 1G intercept course will take us to a matching course 1km from the vessel, ETA 50 minutes."

"Roger, 50 minutes to intercept. Iday, keep scanning as we get closer. Mantis, get all the imagery we can."

In about 30 minutes Iday added, "Very minor power readings and no life signs so far. I'm assuming no atmosphere and no gravity."

As they continued closer Ximon stated, "Matching course and speed. Mantis, put visual on main screen."

A large image of the apparently dead vessel appeared. It was approximately four times the size of the Mantis and was clearly designed for cargo but mounted several weapons. It had several sizable, ragged holes spread along the hull.

"Elsbeth, what do you make of those holes?"

"Hard to say. Looks like meteor strikes to me, but I guess they could be some kind of physical projectile. Iday, what do you think?"

Iday, "I would tend to agree. They don't look like laser blasts, but we'd have to get closer to be sure."

"I think that's exactly what we're going to have to do. Elsbeth, do you see any issue docking with it?"

"No, the airlocks look standard. The doors might be locked, but we should be able to get past that."

"OK, then, beginning docking maneuver, port airlock. All three of you go start suiting up and grab weapons and tools. Make sure your mag boots are engaged. I'll join you as soon as we're docked."

The maneuver went flawlessly, and the airlocks mated up nicely.

Ximon checked his board. "I'm showing a green connection here."

Elsbeth verified on her screen. "Showing green here, but we need to button up."

"Roger, seal up and check each other. Elsbeth, get that door open. Video everything."

"Naturally. I tried knocking, but got no response. Working on the key pad now."

Ximon said, "Mantis, once I get in, keep our airlock closed unless one of us signals you. Continue to monitor the vessel and the general environment and signal me with any issues."

"Yes, Captain."

Elsbeth got the door open before Ximon was ready so the three of them stepped in and started scouting the immediate area.

Elsbeth radioed, "Ok, looks like we're in the passenger quarters area, starting in the aft. No lights, no air, no gravity. Starting to look in the cabins. Moving from aft toward what should be the bridge."

A few seconds later Iday added, "Port 1 clear." They proceed down the hallway, alternating who checked each room.

At Starboard 2, Elsbeth Groaned, "Crap, I didn't need to see that. We've got a floater in Starboard 2. Looks like explosive decompression."

At Port 3, Raiza said, "We have two bodies in Port 3. Apparent decompression."

Shortly thereafter Elsbeth added, "I see the reason. Looks like a hull breach just before the next bulkhead."

They then reached the escape pods. All six were there, but there was a dead body in the sealed pod 5.

Iday said, "Looks like this guy got in the pod but the damage had prevented it from firing. Apparent suffocation."

By this time Ximon had joined them as they got to the bulkhead door.

Iday checked it with his hand scanner. "There's apparently some atmosphere on the other side."

So, they went forward, letting out some very stale atmosphere as they did so. Here, there were five more rooms, apparently crew quarters. They found no bodies in the quarters. They also found three more escape pods and an empty escape pod rack. So, someone had apparently gotten off the ship. But two of the pods were smashed as if someone had attacked them.

Then they proceeded to the bridge. They knocked and got no reply. When they entered the bridge, they again vented trace oxygen. In the bridge, they found two bodies in vacc suits at their stations.

Ximon looked hard at the two bodies and the situation.

"Looks like they used this as their last stand. This section of the ship wasn't exposed to vacuum, but maybe the air recyclers crapped out. Then they got in vacc suits until that oxygen died."

Elsbeth looked and nodded. "Looks like. I've got several expended tanks here. They might have been in their suits for eight to ten hours."

"Probably trying to save her somehow. Ok, let's move down to the cargo deck."

They all climbed down the hatch to the fore cargo deck. The entire cargo area appeared to be vacuum and they found several hull breaches. The hold was full of a variety of crates and they found two bodies floating about, victims of decompression.

They checked the bay where the ship's launch was stored. It didn't look damaged but looked like it had been in the middle of maintenance when the maintainers died.

They searched a few small storage rooms off the cargo bay. No bodies, but they found four empty cryogenic (cryo) chambers in one.

Cryo Chamber: Small, simple, and robust cryogenic chambers used on board ships. They have several uses:

1)   *They allow gravely sick or injured personnel to be frozen until the ship reaches good medical facilities and then unfrozen for good medical care.*
2)   *They allow low-paying passengers to be frozen and then easily unfrozen after a trip. A common space travelling maxim says, "There ain't no passenger less trouble than a frozen passenger."*
3)   *They allow passengers on long-duration voyages to be frozen for the duration, so they do not age. This usage was more common before the jump drive was developed as back then interstellar travel took many years.*

They went back to engineering.

Port engineering had taken a direct hit and there was some damage to both the port power plant and maneuver drive. Starboard engineering had also taken a hit with two dead floating and damage to the maneuver drive. The power plant, however, was operating at a minimal level and some of the monitoring stations were functioning. Elsbeth spent a couple minutes doing some checks.

"Wow! This happened about five months ago, and it looks like the universe decided to really bend them over that day. I think they mis-jumped here and then almost immediately took serious damage with multiple hull breaches. Probably a meteor swarm. They probably came out of jump early, so they weren't ready for regular space. Their starboard fuel tank is low, and the port is dry. So, they probably arrived with just maneuver fuel and then had a tank punctured. It looks like the starboard maneuver drive was knocked offline right away and the port damaged. That might have been usable, but they likely couldn't feed fuel from the starboard fuel tank. Logs make it look they were trying to just use thrusters to adjust course until damage to power couplers knocked those off line. I don't see why more escape pods weren't used, but I'm betting a power junction was hit and they lost hydraulic pressure, so couldn't fire. And their launch was down for maintenance. Like I said, they were screwed about as bad as you can be all at once."

Ximon said, "OK, what do you think?"

Iday said, "We should make some attempt to find that escape pod, perhaps that nearby dwarf planet."

"True, though there's no way they could still be alive if they weren't picked up."

Elsbeth turned to look at them. "Yeah, but if they did get picked up why are we the first to find this?"

"Good question and very important to us as I see it. If that crew member is alive, they may have some claim to salvage. If not, we can definitely claim this."

Iday, "I can't imagine why they wouldn't have filed before now if they made it, but I guess we'll see."

Elsbeth considered options. "So, what's our play?"

Ximon, "Well, first thing is to gather the logs and catalog things."

"Then, I'd like to spend some time taking some parts and tools."

"Right, we'll also need to collect the bodies and some personal effects, and we might as well see if any of the cargo is salvageable and I'd like to try to take the weapons from the mounts. Oh, and I want to take at least a few of those cryo chambers if they look workable. They're real useful to have when you're flying about on the edge of things."

"That'll all take some time, at least a day. Should I steal engine parts too or are you thinking salvage?"

"Well that depends. In a while here, I'll send a salvage claim. Then we can start doing all that. It'll take a while to hear back. If it's denied, then I vote we take engine parts and that launch. If our claim is validated, then we can leave them and hope to make up the money in salvage. Thoughts?"

Iday cut in, "Sounds reasonable. Unless we can find a way to make some sections airtight and fill them with air, we're going to have to watch our air carefully and make frequent trips back to Mantis. Though we can reduce that by bringing every spare air tank we have over here."

Elsbeth continued looking at her screen. "I'll look to see if we can mate our cargo door with one of theirs. If so, we may want to reconnect after we get some of the stuff from this deck. Recommend we bring a couple carts and you all start loading them up from here."

"OK, Elsbeth, you go check the door and oxygen options. Iday and Raiza, please gather the bodies from the upper deck and put them all in the first cabin by the air lock, and those from the lower by the cargo door. Then go through the cabins and look for stuff to put in two piles: significant personal affects matching those bodies, and stuff that can be of use, value, or interest to us. I'll hit the bridge and get all the flight logs so I can get those to Mantis and have her start analyzing."

They went about their respective chores. Elsbeth said they could match cargo doors. Ximon sent the logs to Mantis and then helped Iday and Raiza. Then they all brought the odds and ends to Mantis. They had a sizable, catalogued pile of personal effects and personal comm units and tablets. They also had a pile of stuff of interest including a few weapons, a couple sets of personal armor, six vacc suits (without bodies in them), and electronics. They unloaded it and then rested in Mantis for a while and recharged their air.

Then Ximon sent a salvage claim to Zulea Prima Station, claiming the ship as salvage since it had been abandoned for an extended period of time. He also had Mantis search for towing tug options.

Mantis had already gotten some info from the dead ship's logs.

"The ship is the Peregrine Galley. It operated out of the Qai system, approximately 97 light years away. The manifest shows eight crew and four passengers. I've sent you the names to match to the bodies and possessions. I've also sent you the cargo manifest.

"The ship mis-jumped here on day 128 and sensor logs indicate they emerged from jump surrounded by a substantial meteor swarm. The immediately took multiple hits. The captain and second mate were on the bridge and tried in vain to save the ship. They sent distress calls, but the primary comms array was damaged. The messages probably had short range and limited arc. Logs do show one escape pod getting away with someone on board, but then multiple system failures prevented further launches. The captain tried to modify the ship's course by using maneuvering jets until those ran out of power or gas. After 20 hours and 32 minutes, the ship shows the captain unresponsive."

Ximon took all that in and answered, "Thank you, Mantis. Please start putting together a draft lost vessel report. Please also analyze the data from the recovered personal comms devices to see if anything there can add to the account. Let me know when you hear anything back on that salvage claim."

"I will captain, but at our distance round trip time is almost nine hours."

"Oh, and did the logs give a trajectory or other information on that pod?"

"Only an initial vector. It was heading in the general direction of Zulea Sub 1, which was passing through that area at that time. If nothing changed the vector, the pod would have gotten fairly close to Zulea Sub 1's moon."

They took a bit of a rest and Ximon and Iday examined the cargo manifest.

Ximon warned everyone, "Roger. Everyone have a seat. Now I'm going to maneuver to connect our cargo hatch to theirs."

Once joined, they suited back up, worked through that airlock, and brought a few carts.

"Elsbeth, gather up tools and spares. Do you need a hand?"

"It'd go faster."

"Ok, Raiza please assist. Iday, you're with me. We'll

examine the stuff in the secure cargo area and forward cargo bay first. We'll reposition the interesting stuff back here and then take it all at once."

They reconvened in about 90 minutes and moved the interesting stuff across. In addition to quite a few tools and spare parts, they had recovered some interesting cargo items. This included: two crates of personal weapons and ammo, two crates of physical mail, a crate of luxury clothes, a crate of personal electronics, and two crates of small manufactured goods. They also wheeled across three of the four cryo chambers.

They all unsuited and had a good meal, then discussed next steps.

Ximon, "Elsbeth, you'll need to do a spacewalk to investigate the ship's weapons and recover what's salvageable. I assume you'll want a hand?"

"Yes. In zero G they're light, but they're still big an awkward. Iday, can you help? You know ship's weapons better than me."

Iday nodded his assent. "Of course."

Ximon was glad to hear it coming together. "OK. Get on it. Raiza and I will move bodies to their cargo bay. We won't move them to Mantis until we're ready to leave – they won't all fit in the fridge or the cryo chambers."

Suited back up again, Ximon and Raiza went to the other ship and carefully lowered the upper deck bodies down the access hatch from the top deck to the lower deck. Then they laid them out neatly on a pallet near the cargo door.

As they were doing so, Elsbeth reported, "OK, Ximon, here's what we've got. There's a double turret with 2 light laser cannons that don't appear significantly damaged, a fixed chaff thrower that looks damaged and we don't need, and a mounted light laser cannon that looks damaged but fixable. I propose we just get the entire turret at this time, all right?"

"That sounds good. I'll try to open one of the side cargo doors and clear space."

About two hours later, they'd gotten the turret into the ship and then hauled it over to the Mantis. Then they returned to the Mantis and rested.

Mantis informed Ximon, "I received an acknowledgement of the salvage claim. It indicated that no immediate counter-claim was indicated."

"Woot woot! It's only a start, but that's great!"

"I have also sent you a list of potential tugs for hire. Would you like me to request one of them?"

"Yes, request the one that can get here the fastest and has good ratings for reliability and skill."

"Yes, Captain."

Elsbeth looked up with interest. "Ximon, we'll need that tug, but I have an idea that might help. I think I can recharge their maneuver jets and we could use them to adjust the course, so it's headed a bit more sunward. I'd guess we could get about 10 to 12 degrees change per fill. That would lessen the recovery time a bit and start building toward a fallback option."

"OK, we've got quite a wait, anyway. Give it a try, and let's see how it goes after the first fill."

Ximon then announced more generally. "I think we've got to check near Zulea Sub 1 for any sign of that pod. I can't think of any way they could be alive unless they were recovered, but it would be nice to know whether or not they are alive. Per the manifest the guy that escaped, Arend Daling, was the navigator. Without knowing their contract, we don't know whether he might have a right to claim salvage as a surviving ship's officer."

Iday looked somewhat skeptical. "But if he was going to

do that, one would think he would already have done so and would have filed it in this system."

"I agree, but who knows? Anyway, we need to at least look. It would only be a five hour round trip to Zulea Sub 1. Would y'all agree we should go after Elsbeth tries the jets a time or two?"

Iday shrugged his shoulders. "That sounds reasonable. We don't have an ETA for the tug, but it will certainly be at least 60 to 80 hours."

"That sounds good, but we could instead just leave me here," Elsbeth said. "I'd have plenty of air and several spare tanks, even a spare suit or two. I could do the maneuver jets several times and could also check a few more things in engineering."

Ximon was a bit taken aback, surprised at the idea. "I don't like the idea of leaving someone here."

"I'll be OK, and you can leave Raiza to protect me and to ensure you don't forget me. It goes without saying that if you leave me my ghost will kill you in your sleep."

Ximon smiled at that. "That's not a bad idea if you're sure you're comfortable with that."

"Sure. I was needing some 'girl time.'"

Ximon turned to Raiza, "Raiza, what do you think?"

"Whatever will best serve you and the ship, captain."

"Ok then. Let's get the gear you need to do the jets a few times. Then, I'll plot that course at a quick burn."

When the others left, he grabbed Raiza's hand to stop her. He held her close, kissed her, and said, "You're a valuable member of this crew and one hell of a woman."

"Ximon, I'm not actually a woman, nor technically a member of your crew."

"Raiza, you're the only woman for me and the captain gets to say who is and isn't in the crew."

"Thank you Ximon."

"Be careful over there."

This all went smoothly and soon Ximon and Iday were burning at 2.5G for Zulea Sub 1 to shorten the time.

Ximon used a laser designator to highlight stuff on the screen. "We'll do an orbit of each of the moons. Get all the scans you can, both for the pod and general planetary stuff. Then, we'll do one equatorial orbit and one longitudinal orbit of the planet. The planet is small, and the moons are tiny, so it won't take long."

Moon one yielded nothing interesting and was little more than a big rock shaped like potato. Moon 2 was quite a bit larger and had more potential, but they saw nothing. The planet was geologically interesting and Iday almost immediately thought he'd found something. However, it turned out to be a probe that had been sent there years before. But as they came around the other side of the planet, they found what appeared to be the pod tracing a slow orbit.

They plotted a matching course and speed and examined it at close range. The pod was severely damaged, and they noted no life signs. It appeared the guy had escaped his ship only to be killed by the same meteors that had done it in.

Ximon had Iday maneuver just slightly in front of the pod's arc while he tried to retrieve it with the cargo arm. This proved quite difficult, but Ximon got it after several attempts and dragged it into the cargo bay.

He radioed the girls. "We've found the pod and are on our way back. How are y'all doing?"

Raiza answered for them. "We are well. Elsbeth is currently wrestling a hose."

"I see. We'll be back in about 80 to 90 minutes. Stay safe."

A few minutes later Elsbeth signaled Ximon. "I got that under control, we're using the jets for the 3rd time. We're getting about nine degrees course mod each time. That's actually pretty good. Anyway, you can't leave us hanging – is the guy alive?"

"No, looks like the meteor swarm killed him right after he escaped the ship. I feel sorry for him, but it should improve our claim. We were able to retrieve the pod though that was no small feat."

"No doubt. You're hopeless on that arm."

"Well, we got the pod. See you soon."

Mantis informed them, "The tug Cesar Muros is schedule to leave Zulea 5 in five hours and should meet us in approximately 90 hours. We'll need to send an updated path for the salvage when we finish with the jets."

So, then they waited. They did the jets a few more times but were getting diminishing returns. They just weren't used to such sustained use and some had died. Elsbeth spent some time working on the launch. She was able to get it mostly put back together and did some diagnostics on it, but something was wrong with its maneuvering drive. It would take more time than they had and would be infinitely easier without a space suit. While she messed with that everyone else did another pass of the ship to ensure they didn't miss anything. They moved the bodies to the Mantis shortly before the tug arrived.

The tug arrived at the updated intercept point about an hour later than expected, but soon got to work getting the Peregrine Galley under tow. It would take them almost 80 hours to get to a dry dock at Zulea Prima, so the Mantis went on a little ahead.

On the way to Zulea Prima, Mantis encountered a couple intra-system cargo shuttles, a passenger shuttle, a small yacht, and a Zulean system defense boat (SDB). The SDB captain, in particular, was quite friendly. He was glad to see a KSF ship and interested in the data Mantis has collected since they jumped in. He was also quite interested in their story of pirates in Cruna Sigma (lest they decide to try things here). He gave Ximon a link to another job source that might not be readily available and told Ximon he could say, "Captain Grayson sent you."

As they headed in, Ximon arranged for a slot in the dry dock, a ship inspector, and a cargo broker to come inspect the cargo and sell what he could. Saddest of all, Ximon (regretfully) hired a lawyer to monitor their salvage claim since it might take longer than they were willing to hang out in Zulea. Finally, he finished and sent the Lost Ship report to Station Security and filed a copy with their salvage claim.

They had already landed and turned the bodies and personal effects over to security before the tug laboriously put the ship in the dry dock. Ximon sent the Cesar Muros the (seemingly exorbitant) fee and thanked them. Then he had Iday work with the cargo broker, while Elsbeth had the launch moved to a dock where she could work on it and searched for some necessary parts or repairs for the Mantis.

He took Raiza with him to go see the lawyer. They laid out the situation and provided him a summary of all the logs, plus their imagery. He seemed to think they had a fairly solid case but had to investigate what the owners of the ship had done when it went missing. Interstellar communication being what it was, he thought they'd have an answer in about two months. Ximon said they'd be in system for at least a week in case any questions came up before then.

Ximon invited everyone to meet them for dinner at a nice restaurant and they all summarized what they'd found. Iday reported that the cargo buyer should have an estimate the next day. Ximon summarized the lawyer's views. Everyone was interested in that potential windfall.

Elsbeth reported on her search for jump coil options. "Ok, Ximon, their part options are *not* great, and the prices are not exactly cheap. I can get individual components that should … SHOULD … allow me to repair the coil. They're about 4,000, it would take me about eight hours in port to do, and there's little guarantee how long it would last. Alternately, I've got a line on a refurbished coil that should work. That's about 12,000 and would take me about four hours to replace. Which one should I try?"

"See if you can get the refurbished one. Do you need a hand?"

"Will do, but I'm keeping the bad one and I'm going to want to get those component parts when we get back home so we have an actual working spare. I could use an extra set of hands while doing the repair – you, Raiza, or some hot young stud, preferably the latter."

"Spares – novel idea. I'll help you tomorrow or the next day. Other than that, everyone, take a few days off. We'll target a launch at 0700 in four days. I'll start checking on possible jobs in-system and enroute back home and will update you on timing."

JAUNT 5: ON THE MANTIS EXPRESS

Ximon spent a little time looking at job feeds before deciding to turn it over. "Mantis, please check the job feeds. Gather data on any potential jobs for us. If there are any, I'd like to do a couple jobs within the system. Then look for any jobs -- cargo, passengers, survey, etc. that takes us – Tixaya, Thade X, or Cepheo systems."

"Yes, Captain. I will consolidate and prioritize that data. Please note that the primary station for interstellar trade is in orbit of Zulea Prima, there are also substantial mining and agricultural colonies on planet, as well as two based on Zulea Prima's primary moon and one on her secondary. There are also several smaller bases on other planets or moons in the system. Would you like me to check all sites?"

"Yes, please."

Ximon then asked Raiza to join him. "Raiza, please, come sit with me." She came and sat on his lap. Though her frame and many components were metal, they were high-tech alloys, so she weighed very similar to a human female of her size and she was fairly petite. He wasn't sure, but he thought that she could lock her tendons in such a way that only a portion of her weight was actually resting on him. So, she was entirely comfortable to have sit there (when the crew wasn't around). She hummed happily because she knew Ximon liked that if he didn't have to concentrate too much on something.

Shortly, Mantis sent Ximon a list of jobs.

"Captain, I have sorted these by payment relative to the

portion of ship capacity they will consume and the alignment with the stated destination systems and an assumed desired departure date. If you'd like I could also attempt to derive a list of possible combinations."

"Thank you, Mantis. Please do."

Ximon scrolled through the list. There was more than he had expected, but none looked especially exciting.

Ximon put together a few options or combinations, but when Mantis provided her options, they were more complete. So, he went of her list and combinations.

It looked like they could possibly do an in-system job in a few days, then take passengers bound for Cepheo, Thade X, and Tixaya, as well as cargo bound for Cepheo and Thade X.

Ximon perused the list one last time and picked several jobs to apply for. The first one was in intra-system job in four days. That'd take them a couple days, then there were cargo and passengers headed the way they wanted to go.

He heard back in about an hour that they'd got the intra-system job, so he updated the crew to report 0800 hours in four days to make ready.

Elsbeth arranged to meet him the next day to install the refurbished coil.

When Elsbeth arrived, she said, "If you can come give me a hand in about 20 minutes, we'll put this in."

The install went pretty smoothly and Elsbeth said initial diagnostics checked out.

I'm going out now, but I'll do some calibration over the next couple days and (assuming you don't do something to make it impossible) on that intra-system flight."

She then added, "Oh, and I fixed that launch. I wish we could keep her, but there's no way she'll fit in the Mantis. So, I guess we should sell her."

Ximon turned over the physical mail for payment and then he and Raiza went through the goods they'd take from salvage. He took a few of the personal electronics as gifts for the crew and had Raiza pick out a few of the luxury clothes for herself.

He bought a bigger weapons locker and stocked it with some of the weapons and ammo they had. He added a few more shotguns, automatic and laser pistols, automatic and laser rifles, and a few suits of armor. He sold the rest of the goods and weapons they'd taken from salvage directly to a reseller. They got some decent money for it all.

He was also able to sell the launch. They were selling fast, it was older, and it had some issues. However, they still got an even 1.9 Mcr! He immediately sent both Elsbeth and Iday a bonus of 100 Kcr each.

Over the next few days, Ximon and Raiza went to restock the galley and some stuff in the rooms the passengers would be using. They especially needed quite a bit more food if they were hauling passengers.

The gathered back at 0800 on the fourth day.

Ximon announced, "Ok, here's the plan. We're running about 25 miners out to Zulea 7. Once we're done there, we'll swing by Zulea 5 and get a handful of passengers and some cargo to bring back here. Then I'll check in with the lawyer and we'll head out on an intersystem job. So, we're going to need to configure the cargo bay for passengers (pax). I know there are stowed seats back there, but we've never used them. I think there are supposed to be 36 seats, so even if a few don't work, there should be enough."

"Iday and Elsbeth, please get on that and ensure that little latrine by the cargo bay is ready to go. Also, try to hook up some kind of screen so we can show a Vid in there."

Elsbeth groaned. "What are we opening a theater now?"

"You know a distracted pax is a less troublesome pax – we're saving ourselves some grief. These pax are going to be limited to the cargo bay, that latrine, the galley, and the head next to it. All other doors should be locked. Raiza and I will get the galley ready with water and some snacks, with sandwiches ready to serve about six hours in. We'll also bring down some water shortly. Get moving, the PAX should arrive by 0940."

"Mantis, you'll need to monitor security camera feeds for non-crew traffic outside those areas."

"Yes, Captain."

Before doing anything else, he had Raiza change into a baggy set of coveralls he'd gotten for her and put on a scout hat. He didn't want her to look too inviting to the miners, male or female.

Then he helped Raiza in the galley.

Just before planned arrival time, Ximon stationed Iday in the galley and Elsbeth in the cargo hold. Ximon waited for the group to arrive, which they did promptly.

There were 24 of them, each with a large duffel. They looked like rough men and women as one would expect. The leader sent Ximon a manifest.

Before he let the first one on board Ximon proclaimed, "Welcome to the Mantis. Our flight should be about 19 hours. I'll check each of you against the manifest and then you'll go in. Your seating is in the cargo bay and you'll stow your bags in a crate there. You'll have the use of the cargo bay and, once we're away from the planet, the galley. They'll be some snacks out in the galley and we'll have a meal for you in about six hours. She's a good ship and we'll get you there safe and sound. Don't cause trouble or attempt to access other portions of the ship. If you cause trouble, you might spend the rest of the flight in an air-lock. If you cause a lot of trouble that airlock might vent."

He knew he wouldn't really vent someone into space just for being a bit unruly, but it was a fairly standard threat.

Then Ximon checked each one off carefully (mostly to space them out on entering the ship) and they all got on board. Ximon scoped out the situation in the cargo bay. It looked pretty good. Almost all of the fold out seats looked good and they had Vid already running.

Ximon made a general announcement. "Hit the head if you need to and then buckle up. We'll be taking off in 15 minutes and there'll be some Gs."

Then he headed for the bridge but had a security feed showing on one of the screens. He and Iday quickly preflighted and got clearance.

Ximon again announced, "Take off in three minutes. Ensure you're strapped."

They got going fast after that. As soon as they got away from the planet, Ximon and Iday took turns meandering through the galley and cargo bay. Most of the miners were snoozing or mindlessly watching the vid. A few hung out in the galley, one small group playing some obscure game. They seemed to be behaving themselves well. Raiza and Ximon took the sandwiches down after a few hours and they all ate.

A while later some of the miners started a fight in the cargo bay and Ximon was alerted. Ximon announced to the cargo bay, "This is the captain. Get in your seats now."

When a few of them kept screwing around, Ximon quickly announced, "You're losing artificial gravity."

Thirty seconds later, with no sign of them complying, Ximon had Mantis cut the gravity just in the cargo bay. The few who didn't get strapped in tended to slam into things. They quickly got the point and got in their seats. Ximon turned it back on in about 30 minutes and they were all good after that.

The rest of the flight was uneventful, and they were all

strapped in about 30 minutes prior to landing. Ximon landed her on the designated landing pad on a desolate looking moon. A passenger tunnel snacked out and mated to their airlock and Iday had them line up and head out. The leader digitally signed the manifest as proof of delivery, and they were gone. Ximon took off within ten minutes and Raiza and Iday cleaned stuff up on the way to Zulea 5.

Along the way Elsbeth reported, "I got the calibration and some additional tests done. I think we're good to jump."

They radioed the station at Zulea 5 when they were 30 minutes out and then landed and mated up with a cargo tunnel. The few pallets of stuff were loaded within ten minutes and then the Pax got on. These guys were in for a shorter flight (about seven hours), were tired, and were anxious to get to Zulea Prima. Within the main station there, there was "civilization," which to many of them probably meant hotels, showers, restaurants, gambling, and brothels. Who was he to judge?

Mantis got back to Zulea Prima station without incident and everyone and everything got unloaded fast. It was about 1100.

Ximon then announced to the crew, "OK, we've got cargo loading tomorrow at 1800. Iday can you manage that?"

Iday nodded.

"Then we've got pax coming at 0600 the next day for a 0630 take off. So, again, let's huddle at 0500."

The cargo loading was uneventful – about ten crates of manufactured goods, two crates of physical mail, and three crates of specialty shipping items. The cargo bay was quite full.

Ximon checked in with the lawyer the next day. He had no updates but got a few more details from Ximon.

When they huddled the next day Ximon briefed the crew.

"Ok, we're heading for the Cepheo system. This time we've got these pax for weeks, so they'll be in cabins four, five, and six, and they'll be sharing the same communal showers. We'll have alternating hours for men and women with an automated sign – read it and heed it!"

"In number four, we've got some kind of business man, in number five, a small family (mama, daddy, and baby) that's bringing a small portable crib, in number six is a young couple. Obviously, we need to be more gracious with this lot. Raiza, you'll be serving three meals a day (0600, 1200, and 1800) and should be on duty in the galley an hour before each and all call except for 2200 to 0400. All the rest of us will help and we'll be happy helpers. Everyone keep clean coveralls on when you're in those galley area. No walking around half naked, drunk, or killing anyone. Got me?"

Elsbeth and Iday just nodded.

Raiza said, "Of course captain. I am happy to help. If necessary, I can be on call 24 hours. I don't need to sleep."

"Raiza, you need charge and maintenance time and you'll occasionally be needed for other duties. They can choose to sleep then or just not be needy."

Ximon heard Elsbeth snort and say under her breath, "Other duties."

He gave her a glare and she just gave an innocent smile.

They got everything ready for the pax. These passengers were somewhat less orderly. The young couple, the Dahves, arrived at 0545. They both appeared to be naïve 20-somethings, anxious to start a new life on Thade X and barely able to keep their hands off each other. The family, the Kollars, arrived at 0600. They were an average-looking couple pushing 40 with a baby about a year old. They mainly just looked tired. The business man, Alfur Ulfson, rushing up at 0625. He was the stereotypical middle-aged businessman, well dressed for space travel, but too self-important to be on time. Elsbeth and Raiza rushed him to his room while Ximon and Iday got ready to take off. Each room had a couple flip-down seats that they could buckle into or they could strap into their bed.

They took off without incident and headed for their jump point and then the pax's personalities emerged.

The family's baby seemed to cry a lot if they were either under acceleration and when they went briefly into zero G. The walls were fairly thick, so it wasn't too bad, but the business man did seem to get annoyed. During the jump they arranged things so the mom or dad could take the baby down to the cargo bay. The noises there seemed to calm it. At one point the parents had some kind of accident in the galley and had their hands full. Without thinking, the mom handed the baby to Raiza who was standing nearby. Ximon happened to be cutting through the galley and was most amused to see Raiza awkwardly holding a baby. It was very clear she had no training in child rearing or even child holding. He smiled at her as he went by.

The young couple only seemed to emerge from their room to eat or use the shower. Despite the gender-oriented hours and signs, they tried to use the shower together at least once. However, since it's a communal shower room, at least one of them was in there at the wrong time. One time they were getting VERY frisky when Iday came in. Everyone was quite embarrassed. To avoid a recurrence Ximon changed the shower times so that each group of passengers (Ulfson, Kollars, and Dahves) could have a private 30-minute block at 2200, 2230, and 2300 or use the gender-designated times. However, Ximon only noted that the Dahves used their "private time," and they used it EVERY SINGLE DAY.

The jump to Cepheo was uneventful other than some interesting conversations and occasional annoyances. The baby did seem to cry a lot and the parents got frustrated. The others mostly stayed to themselves.

When they got to Cepheo, Ximon was happy to see a message from the lawyer back on Zulea Prima. He said that the owners of the Peregrine Galley had contested the salvage and had offered a relatively small reward instead. Per Ximon's directions, he had declined the offer. He was confident that, given the precedence of salvage laws and the owners' insurance claim against the ship, that Ximon's claim would stand.

They dropped cargo without incident and the Kollars departed. They also took on a few passengers. Lady Constance Iauxia, a middle-aged minor noble of something or other, and her maid Thuvia Ivanova, a petite, attractive, 20-something woman. Those two would be sharing a room and a bed. Ximon had made that abundantly clear to the booking agent, but Lady Iauxia was fine with the arrangement. Ximon thought to himself, "Who am I to judge? I'm sleeping with a hot bot."

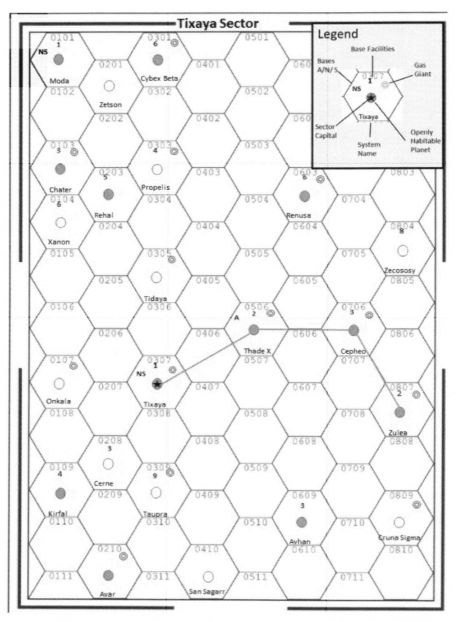

They also had two passengers come on for Cryo passage, being frozen all the way to Tixaya. The first was a grandfatherly old guy in his 60s or 70s named Elihu Cord. The second was a 30-ish, wanna-be rock star named Slade Fazio who seemed quite arrogant and surprised that they hadn't heard of him. Iday, who had the most medical experience, took them back to the storage room of the cargo bay where they had installed the cryo chambers. Then he 'tucked them in' with a brief "Good night" and a prayer. The process was pretty simple, but he was a bit nervous. He had practiced it several times over the last few days under Mantis' careful tutelage.

Ximon and Raiza got the other passengers settled, stowed their (considerable) luggage, and informed them of the shower schedule and meal times. Ximon hoped that "Lady Constance" wasn't going to be too much of a pain to Raiza or the rest of them. Time would tell.

Ximon, Iday, and Elsbeth did their respective system checks and pre-flights. Everything looked good to go and they took off 20 minutes later, headed for a jump point to Thade X.

Lady Constance was, indeed, a bit of a pain. She complained at the meals and asked for special stuff which they obviously didn't have. Ximon felt bad for Raiza, though he knew she didn't mind.

Ximon finally told Lady Constance, "Ma'am, please be patient and understanding. Our cook here is doing the best she can with the standard fair we stock. You have booked passage on a small scout ship, not a luxury liner."

Lady Constance also had an annoying habit of repeatedly asking the same questions of anyone around. She asked Ximon at least three times when they'd be jumping, though the answer didn't change, and he found out later that she had also asked Iday, Raiza, and Elsbeth. Once in jump she asked when they'd be out of jump repeatedly. Eventually Ximon had Raiza put their planned jump and arrival times on a screen in the galley. Once that was place, every time she asked those same questions the crew would pointedly look at the screen and tell her exactly what it said.

They entered jump without incident and the crew went about mundane tasks and occasional passenger handling.

The Dahves spent most of their time in their room and were hugging or holding hands when they weren't there. Ulfson was seen even less, only leaving his room for meals (which he rushed through) and brief showers. Lady Constance and Thuvia, on the other hand, seemed to haunt the galley. They read, ate, talked, and watched vids there.

At meals, The Dahves talked mostly to each other, Ulfson talked little or none and seemed in a rush, Lady Constance talked to everyone, almost as if she was holding court. Thuvia said nothing unless directly questioned. She spoke with a strange, heavy accent and Standard clearly wasn't her first language. So Ximon wasn't sure if her silence was because she was self-conscious about her speech or if it was because she didn't think it was 'her place' to speak in mixed company.

Things progressed like this for a couple days.

On day three of the jump, Mantis signaled Ximon privately. "Captain, I'm concerned about Mr. Ulfson. He has missed the last three meals and security cameras do not show him leaving his room for 27.45 hours."

"That is odd. I noticed he wasn't at dinner, but now that you mention it, he wasn't at breakfast or lunch either. I assumed he just came by the galley and got food some other time. Have you confirmed with Raiza? Perhaps the cameras 'glitched' somehow."

"Yes, captain. In thoroughness, I compared my data from the security feeds with her observations from her time on duty in the galley. She confirmed that he hasn't been in the galley in almost 29 hours, at least while she was on duty. I am concerned that Mr. Ulfson could be ill. Should I do something to address this?"

"No, let me try old-fashior.

So Ximon went to Ulfson's r.
into the intercom. "Mr. Ulfson, excu.
is the captain and we were concerned y
anything we can get you?"

There was no answer or responding ι

Ximon checked again in an hour, wit.   ⸺κ of
results.

So, he went to the bridge and directed Mantis, "Mantis, please note in the log that we are overriding Mr. Ulfson's privacy based on a pressing medical concern. Activate the camera in his room."

The room had no lights on except a small safety light. Ximon couldn't tell much, but Ulfson was clearly lying in bed on his back. He wasn't moving and it looked like he was lying in a puddle of something.

Ximon pounded on the arm of his seat. "Override his door, I'm heading there now. Iday, join me in cabin number four right now!"

Ximon ran down the hallway and opened the now-un-locked door. As he had seen, the room was fairly dark, but light from the hallway lit it fairly well. Ulfson lay sprawled on his back in the bed and it looked like he was covered in a consider-able amount of blood.

Ximon stepped in, closed the door, and turned on the lights. Ximon checked and Ulfson was quite cold and very much dead. There was a lot of blood on his stomach and wrists and the bed was soaked with bed below his arms and torso.

"Oh, god. This is pretty clearly THE last thing we need."

Ximon took a bunch of video. He also told Mantis, "Man-tis, record everything in this room until I tell you differently."

Iday arrived a couple minutes later and knocked. Ximon

sed the door. Iday was in sweats and bare feet, ...veled.

"Iday, Mr. Ulfson is dead. Can you look at him and see what you think?"

Though it was clearly fruitless, Iday checked Ulfson for pulse and breathing. Then he carefully looked at every part of the body.

"Ximon, I'm not a doctor. I can't say anything for sure other than that he's definitely dead."

"We're in mid-jump and you're the best we have. What do you think?"

"It looks like he's been stabbed two to three times in the abdomen and had his wrists cut. I would guess he bled out."

"Anything else?"

"I'm not sure. There are some marks by his mouth that could be bruising, so perhaps someone covered his mouth. Again, I can't be sure."

"So, what do you think happened?"

"Ximon, if forced to guess, it appears he was murdered."

Ximon rubbed his head in frustration. "Great! Just great! Now what the hell do we do?"

"Ximon, normally I would suggest that we just place the body in a cryo chamber and let the authorities on Thade X investigate. However, if my assumption is correct, we have a murderer on the Mantis, and we will be in jump with them for several more days. I would suggest that calls for more immediate action."

Ximon massaged his head as if he had a severe headache (though he almost never got them). "Oh crap, oh crap, oh crap! This isn't in the handbook."

"What handbook would that be?"

"The mythical handbook of what to do when you're running a starship. Ok, let me think."

Ximon and Iday both stared down at the body for a couple minutes. "What else can you find out with the medical analysis unit (MAU)?"

"I'm not entirely sure. I can do some scans and extensive imaging. They might tell us something and, even if they don't, we can present the data to the authorities. Then I suggest we put him in cryo chamber."

"Ok, get the MAU and get to work. Do not say anything to ANYONE. I'll be back in a few."

"Yes, Ximon."

Ximon stepped out went to the galley and took Raiza's hand. She smiled up at him. "What can I do for you Ximon?"

"Come with me for a minute."

He took Raiza to their room and just held her. This thing was really freaking him out. Thoughts of legal problems, lawsuits, scandal, and ruin ran through his mind. Holding her helped him calm them and breathe easier.

Raiza started to say something but detected that wasn't what Ximon needed. So, she began to hum softly, which she knew he found quite comforting.

After a couple minutes he kissed her. "Thank you, dear. You are a great comfort to me."

"That is my fondest desire, my love. What is troubling you and how can I assist? Would you like to make love?"

He smiled at her. "What would I do without you? No love now, but I'll definitely have some frustration to work out later. We've got a serious problem with one of the passengers ..."

She interrupted with some alarm, "Mr. Ulfson? Mantis queried me about his movements. Have I failed in my stewardly duties?"

"No, you're perfect as always. Yes, it's Ulfson. I'll tell you more later, but we've got a problem and I was just … uh … overwhelmed with worry."

"I am here to ease your burdens. Is there anything at all I can do to assist?"

"Not right now. Go back to the galley and don't say anything. I may need your help in a little while. When's lunch?"

"Not for 85 minutes. Should I get you something now?"

"No, thanks. Just wanted to know when we'll likely see the other passengers. Let's go."

He took Raiza's hand and led her back to the galley and then rejoined Iday in Ulfson's room.

Iday had the MAU set up, an internal imager over Ulfson's torso and a few wires and tubes hooked up.

"So, what does it say?"

"I'm still trying to interpret that. He doesn't show any broken bones in the areas with the wounds but shows some old breaks in other bones. The lack of broken/bruised ribs is a little surprising – with those gut wounds, I'd think there would be. That and the MAU measurements, suggest they weren't very forceful. The MAU suggests that the likely blood loss from those alone wouldn't have killed him any time soon, though sepsis might have done so. The MAU shows that his lungs and airways were a bit low of oxygen, so with the facial bruising that might indicate that someone tried to smother him. Can't tell whether that was first or last. His wrists were definitely slit, and that bleeding alone COULD have killed him, but again I can't tell whether he was stabbed in the gut first and then his wrists slit or vice versa."

"OK. So, is there anything else we can do to investigate?"

"Not that I know of. However, the MAU did indicate

that he's got a few chronic conditions, notably heart disease and early stage cancer. Obviously, those didn't kill him, but they might have eventually. The MAU shows no signs of a heart attack or a stroke. His blood alcohol was a bit high and he had some kind of mild sedative in his system. The MAU estimates the time and death at 2200 last night +/- two hours based on blood and tissue changes.

"Do you think he was drugged?

"I can't tell. He could have been, or it could be self-medication."

"So, correct me if I'm wrong – we know that someone stabbed him, slit his wrists, and apparently tried to smother him. But nothing indicates which was first and no clue whatsoever who did this. Right?"

"Yes, I do not know how to determine anything else. I imagine a medical examiner can, but I can't."

"Ok, thanks. I'll have Raiza watch for the other passengers. Let's move him to a cryo chamber so whichever medical examiner wants him can have him."

Ximon grabbed Raiza and had her act as blocker in the hallway, diverting any other passengers while they carried the body to the cargo bay. They got there figure out to do from here forward."

Ximon went to the bridge and discussed with the Mantis.

"Mantis, please analyze activity on the security feeds for the last 48 hours. Make timelines of the movements of every passenger AND crew member. In particular, I want to know anyone who ever passed by Ulfson's room."

"Roger, captain. I have most of that compiled. I will complete the analysis and timeline within a few minutes."

Ximon just sat down and thought to himself, "How can I

solve this? I'm not cop – what would they do? What are the authorities on Thade going to want to do or want from us?" Again, he started to envision a lot of potential problems.

Mantis seemingly read his mind. "Captain, you might find KSF Manual J-065, Handbook for Criminal Investigative Officers, useful. While it is not specifically focused on investigations under these conditions, it discusses investigations of this type and provides suggestions which may prove helpful. I've sent it to your tablet and marked several sections that may be useful."

Ximon hadn't thought of that. "Thank you. I'll look at that."

A few minutes later, Mantis showed him everything he had asked for. Almost everything looked reasonable. For the most part, none of the passengers went anywhere other than their room, the galley, and the showers. The one bizarre exception to that was the maid, Thuvia -- she twice went down to the room with the cryo chambers in the middle of the night. In theory, she shouldn't have been able to even get there, but an unlocked door wasn't too unlikely. The crew, of course, was all over the ship, but that was as they'd expected.

As far as Ulfson's room, until Ximon knocked, it didn't look like anyone but him ever touched his door, though some of the passengers and crew walked past it.

There was nothing here to suggest that anyone went in Ulfson's room nor that he was attacked anywhere else, though the maid thing was odd.

Ximon plugged in a personal tablet so Mantis could detect it. "Mantis, this is Mr. Ulfson's personal tablet. Please see if you can find any information on it that may tell us something."

"Captain, I will attempt to do so, though I do not believe that is ideal chain of custody procedure. The device is also clearly encrypted. I am not sure what I can find."

"Very well, but see what you can find."

"Yes, captain."

Ximon took a minute to review Mantis' summaries of key sections of the investigation handbook. She had been correct that it was focused differently, but he did get some ideas, questions to ask, etc.

He summoned the entire crew, including Raiza, to the bridge. It took a couple of minutes for them to get there. Iday looked a little more presentable, but Elsbeth looked like she had just rolled out of bed. She wore sweat pants, a t-shirt, and slippers. Her hair was a wreck and she might have been a bit hungover.

She said groggily, "Ximon, why have you woken me out a great dream? You may not know it, but I need my beauty sleep."

Ximon ignored her. "Ok, everyone, shut up and listen. Mantis start recording."

He continued, "This is Captain Ximon Sabo or the KSS SC-1550-V Mantis. We are currently located in jump space between the Cepheo System and the Thade X System. We have been in jump space for approximately 59 hours. One of our passengers, a Mr. Ulfson, is dead. He apparently died last night at approximately 2200 hours. Cause of death is unclear, but he was stabbed several times in the abdomen, his wrists were slit, and there may have been an attempt at smothering.

"The body was found by me at 0830 hours after the ship computer noted that the passenger had not been seen for an extended period of time. Upon initial review it was abundantly clear that he was dead. Sensor Operator Idayvo Oretes, having the most medical knowledge, has examined the body with the Medical Analysis Unit and determined the approximate time of death, also that he had a few chronic conditions, but that none of them appear to have killed him. It was unclear which wound was fatal. No murder weapon has yet been found and we, as yet, have no suspects nor motive.

"Since the situation suggests the presence of an active criminal on this vessel and no other authorities can presently be contacted, per Republic law and KSF regulations, as captain, I will act as the initial investigating officer before turning the body and all information obtained over to the first recognized legal authority capable of addressing the matter.

"Mantis, the ship's computer, has already done initial analysis of the ship security feeds and constructed a timeline of passenger and crew movements. Thus far there is no indication of any activity relevant to Mr. Ulfson's death.

"I will begin the investigation by preparing my own statement and taking statements from the crew individually. Our engineer will immediately conduct an inspection of all security systems for error or manipulation and will tender me a report.

"Mantis has assembled the following information about Mr. Ulfson ...."

He then turned to let Mantis speak. "This is ship's computer, Mantis. Mr. Alfur Ulfson was taken on as stateroom passenger at the Station at Zulea Prima at 0625 on day 252 with passage to Tixaya, his stated home of record. His passage was arranged by passenger accommodation service SeeZulea. Per regulation, I sent a query to the state instance of the Republic traveller database. His station security documents suggest that he had been on Zulea Prima Station for 11 days, with stated purpose as 'business.' His occupation is stated as fiduciary adviser."

Ximon continued, "This is Captain Sabo. I will conduct and record crew interviews and then question the other passengers. Out."

Mantis quit recording in the official case file.

Ximon continued less formally, "Ok, Elsbeth, the security feeds give us nothing. I need you to do an analysis of them

ASAP for glitches, problems or tampering and send me a written report."

Elsbeth nodded. "Rog, shouldn't be hard."

Ximon then turned to Iday. "Iday, the security feeds did show one strange thing – the maid Thuvia visited the cryo chamber room several times. Check those cryo chambers and make sure those passengers are ok. This may have nothing to do with anything, but it's weird. Oh, and everyone keep all doors that passengers shouldn't use locked."

"The most important thing right now is ship, crew, and passenger safety. I have no clue what happened, but we're stuck in jump for a few days with a murderer. I don't want anyone or anything else hurt. From this moment until we catch someone or land, someone is to be on duty in that galley at all times, with a sidearm. The ship security system SHOULD catch anything, but it doesn't appear that's foolproof so the person there will act as a second set of eyes. Raiza, that will be you most of the time, but one of us will replace you if you're needed elsewhere."

"Iday as soon as you're done checking those cryo chambers, please relieve Raiza. I'll take her statement at that time."

"Oh, and Elsbeth, before you take off, what can you tell us about the garbage system?"

Elsbeth looked incredulous. "The GARBAGE system?"

"Yes, the garbage system."

"Not something I've played with much, but basically all physical waste from any of the rooms goes down a little chute to a compactor. It's then compacted whenever it reaches a certain level, typically every three to four days. The compacted cubes of trash are then either ejected in deep space or turned over for recycling at a station. Any trash since we left the planet will be in the system, but I can't say whether it's been compacted yet or not."

"Check it and if it hasn't compacted yet, turn it off. We

haven't found a murder weapon yet. So, I'm looking for a knife."

"OK. I'll let you know."

Ximon went to the bridge and asked Raiza to come back as soon as Iday relieved her. Ximon took a few minutes to further review the handbook.

Iday messaged him, "The cryo chambers and their passengers appear perfectly fine. I see no sign of tampering. However, someone has placed a picture of Slade on his cryo chamber and it has a heart drawn on it."

"What the heck?"

"Yes, odd. I was careful not to touch it as it could be evidence. I've sent you a picture though."

Then Elsbeth messaged him. "Ximon, the garbage hasn't compacted yet and I've shut it off. Checking the security system now."

Raiza returned several minutes later, "Ximon, how can I be of assistance? Are your further stressed?"

"Oh, I'm stressed, but I need you to witness my video statement and then I will take yours."

"Ximon, I'm not sure that I can legally serve as a witness."

"Well, I say you can and you're what they're getting."

"As you say."

Ximon then had Mantis start recording, stated his name, position and such for the record. Then Mantis asked him some of the recommended questions they had agreed on:

"Captain, how to you know Mr. Ulfson?"

"He is, or was, a passenger on my ship, the Mantis."

"Did you have previous acquaintance with Mr. Ulfson?"

"No"

"Have you ever had any disagreements or altercations with Mr. Ulfson?"

"No"

"Do you have any reason to harm or kill Mr. Ulfson?"

"None"

"Do you know who killed Mr. Ulfson?"

"No, but I am investigating."

"Please describe your movements from 1600 yesterday to 0200 this morning."

Ximon summarized his movements and had Mantis attach the appropriate data from the logs.

"Do you have any further information that may help investigators in determining the cause of Mr. Ulfson's death?"

"Only what I have placed in the case record."

Mantis stated, "Crewmember Raiza, please witness that it was indeed Captain Sabo that gave this statement."

Mantis had a suggested wording up on the screen.

"This is Ship Steward Raiza, of the Mantis. I witness that Captain Sabo provided the preceding statement and was not under duress."

Mantis closed that recording and prepared another.

Ximon turned to Raiza, "OK, now I'm going to take your statement."

Ximon asked her similar questions that Mantis had asked him. Her answers were bland though she had much more insight into Mr. Ulfson's movements.

Ximon then had her send Iday back and repeated the process with him. His answers, of course, reflected that he had investigated the body with the MAU, etc.

Ximon then sent him out and called Elsbeth.

Elsbeth replied, "I'll be right up. I was just going to call you."

Elsbeth appeared looking much more 'put together' and said, "I've sent you a report on the security system. The short answer is there was a glitch for about 48 hours ago – the system hung so no data was recorded. There was then an outage yesterday afternoon for about 30 minutes when I troubleshot the system. It seems to be working fine now and was working fine around the time of the death."

"Ok, I'm going to take your statement now."

Then he went through the same process, including questions about the security system.

"Elsbeth, I'm going to have to ask you and Iday to go through the trash and see if you can find a knife."

Her face modelled fake awe. "Wow – the glory of space travel and all that! Ok, I'll get him and get on it."

Ximon then made an announcement to the passengers. "All passengers, this is Captain Sabo. We are dealing with a matter of extreme urgency. It is essential that you meet me in the galley in 15 minutes – that's at 1125. Lunch will follow thereafter."

He had Raiza go personally knock on their doors to ensure they got the message and that their presence was mandatory. The Dahves were fine, saying, "We were just headed that way."

Lady Iauxia was not happy as she wasn't fully ready and was dressing for lunch at 1200. She just wanted to send her maid, but finally understood that it was a matter of law.

The group assembled in a few minutes, there though not happy. Ximon conducted with a pistol at his hip. Raiza was nearby keeping lunch ready, also wearing a pistol as Ximon had directed.

Ximon dove right in, "Thank you for coming. I've called you here today ..."

Iauxia cut him off and spoke haughtily, "Clearly we are NOT all here. You peremptorily insisted that I attend with virtually no warning, yet that Ulfson fellow isn't here. Is he somehow excused? Is this beneath HIM but not me?"

Ximon worked to not explode. When he spoke his frustration was clear. "Lady Iauxia, we are here because Mr. Ulfson is DEAD! So, yes, he is excused, and I doubt you would like to avail yourself of the same excuse. I would hope you could also excuse our other two passengers that are frozen in sleep."

He then continued more calmly, "Mr. Ulfson died sometime yesterday, and it appears that he may have been killed."

"Murder you mean!?!?"

"Yes, lady, it appears so. We will be in jump for a few more days, so if it is murder, then there is a murderer amongst us."

"Well it is certainly not I ..."

Ximon held up his hand to silence her, which she did not appreciate.

"No other civil authorities can be contacted at this time, so per Republic law and KSF regulations, I as captain am conducting an initial investigation. When we arrive at Thade X, I will turn the case over to them to do as they will but clearly, we cannot simply wait. Our lives and your lives could be in danger."

The Dahves looked somewhat scared and huddled together. The Lady looked irritated and the maid looked confused.

Ximon continued, "So, acting per law, I will interview each of you separately. You will also find that the crew is now armed."

The lady interjected, "Even the *robot*" saying the last word with a stupid emphasis. "Is that quite legal?"

"Lady, Ship Steward Raiza is a member of this crew and I have directed that she be armed for your protection and the protection of this ship. As captain, I have complete discretion as to the security of this ship. Do NOT test me on this!

"We will do everything we can to ensure everyone's safety, but your cooperation is necessary AND required by law. I will now take statements from each of you. Mrs. Dahves, I will start with you, followed by Mr. Dahves, then Lady Iauxia, and finally Thuvia. I have already reviewed all relevant security video and taken statements from the entire crew. Understand that these interviews are official statements and falsehoods will be considered punishable under law and a possible indication of guilt. Ship Steward Raiza will now serve lunch. Mrs. Dahves, please follow me to the cargo hold. Raiza will keep your lunch fresh for you."

Ximon interviewed the young wife. She purported to know nothing of the murder or of Mr. Ulfson other than a few brief conversations at dinner and that he did something with money.

Mr. Dahves was a bit more perceptive and noted that Mr. Ulfson was abrasive and aloof. However, Dahves had had no direct interactions with him other than at dinner and knew of no reason that anyone would want to murder him.

Lady Iauxia clearly had little respect for a "ship driver" acting like a "police person," but answered all the questions. She had opinions of Mr. Ulfson as she had opinions of everyone. She didn't consider him very good company or properly sociable especially since he 'came from money' and clearly 'should have known better.'" But she couldn't see anyone murdering him – "That's just gauche." When asked to account for the movements of her maid she said, "She is my maid and was given errands to attend to such as fetching me tea from the galley, from our room, or such things. She is allowed some free time to read or such on her own and there were a few occasions where she did so. I do NOT track her movements."

The interview with Thuvia was a bit awkward. Her speaking was a bit rough, her accent strong, and she appeared very self-conscious (though that could be guilt). She claimed to know nothing of the murder and only thought of Mr. Ulfson as a 'proper gentlemen.' She had never spoken a word to him. When asked about her relationship with Lady Iauxia she tersely said, "I am her maid."

Ximon felt he need to press this point. "Is there any OTHER relationship?"

The woman blushed beet red and looked down at the table, "I have many close duties to the Lady."

"Are you related? Are you in a relationship?"

"We are not related. We live together as a couple. She is very good to me." Again, she blushed red.

"I understand. Do you think that SHE wanted Mr. Ulfson to come to harm?"

Here she was almost protective. "Of course not. That is beneath her."

"One more question. When you came on board, we made it clear that only your rooms, the galley and the showers were open to passengers and that other areas were off limits. However, our review of security footage shows that you twice entered the restricted cargo bay and then another restricted room. What were you doing there on both occasions?"

She seemed a bit shocked at this turn and looked worried and if she was thinking.

He continued, "Where did you go and why?"

She almost sobbed, "Cryo chambers. I went to the cryo chambers."

"Why, especially when you knew it was restricted?"

"I am sorry, but I love him. I could never get so close. I had to see him. Once I had seen him, I had to return."

"Who did you have to see? Mr. Ulfson? Did you meet him there?"

She looked utterly confused at this and then realized what he was saying.

"No, the great Slade Fazio. I have always loved him and his music. I happened to see him as we were boarding, and I knew I must see him."

"So, you're a big fan of this Fazio?"

"Yes, his songs speak to me."

"What did you do there when you saw him?"

"I looked. I took pictures. You know, selfies. I left a picture, so he would know I loved him."

"Could you show me those pictures please or I'll have to confiscate your phone."

She looked embarrassed as she showed him the pictures. There, indeed, were several pictures of her posing by Slade's cryo chamber, hugging it, kissing it, etc.

"I see. Thank you."

He continued, "Ok, so getting back to Mr. Ulfson, are you saying you know absolutely nothing about his death?"

"Nothing, captain. I am sorry I went where I shouldn't. Will you arrest me now?"

"No, but do not go there again without permission."

Ximon shook his head at that one as he ended the recording. The foreign maid and lover to a lady was a groupie to a nobody rock star and coincidentally chose the time of a murder to do so. There's clearly NO accounting for taste.

About that time Elsbeth reported that after "hours of digging through trash" they had found a knife that they believed was likely the murder weapon.

They stored it away as evidence for the authorities as they had no DNA lab or anything to try to figure out who it belonged to.

Elsbeth then reported to Ximon in person. "I've got something else to tell you. I told you about the security system glitches. It turns out there was another one the night of the murder, but it was quite different. Instead of shutting down the system, it seemed to affect all of the cameras intermittently, different ones at different times, so it was much harder to detect. I've been investigating it and it's very strange. I finally found, and Mantis confirmed, that the security subsystem was affected by a virus. Mantis was able to figure out its sequence of events. Apparently, it deleted itself after causing that glitch. So, apparently someone could have used that time window to enter his room without being seen."

"So, do we know where it came from?"

"Mantis is still checking to be sure, but we think so."

"So, who?"

"It appears to have originated with Ulfson."

Ximon sat up in shock. "WHAT!?!?!?"

"Hold on. That was my reaction – I thought Mantis had blown a gasket. But she traced the installation to his tablet from his room during the flight from Zulea to Cepheo. So, it was definitely before Lady 'high and mighty appeared.' It's hard to see how anyone else could have done it."

"That's still bizarre. Why would he do this?"

"Don't know. Maybe he had something he wanted to do, but someone killed him instead."

"That's not comforting – we had two bad guys on the ship, and one killed the other? And the badder one is still alive? Oh, or do we assume the second one is just an avenging angel?"

Elsbeth just shrugged. "I don't know. You're the investigating officer, but we've taken precautions."

Ximon just rolled his eyes. "Thanks. I'm going to bed."

"What and leave your girlfriend working in the galley? She's been working there all day. I'll give her a break and watch some trashy vids there for an hour or so while keeping watch on our crazy pax."

"Are you sure?"

"Sure. I got your back."

"Thanks."

He took Elsbeth up on the offer and took Raiza to bed for a couple hours. It did a lot to ease frustration and calm him. Ximon fell asleep on her breast, but she somehow managed to sneak out and resume her duties after a couple hours.

Ximon awoke very relaxed the next morning to a communication request from Mantis.

"Yeah."

"Captain, I have some information to pass on to you. Could you come to the bridge at your convenience?"

"Sure, give me ten."

The lovely Raiza gave him a big smile and handed him a cup of coffee and a breakfast sandwich as he came through the galley. "Good morning, Ximon. Mantis told me that you would be visiting her."

That was nice, but a little scary. He'd have to keep in mind that he had two or three, women working together, perhaps against him.

He made it to the bridge and sat down in his seat. "Good

morning, Mantis. What do you have?"

"Two primary things. First, I reviewed Elsbeth's investigation of the virus and the conclusion seems sound. The virus seemed to be intentionally inserted into my security subsystem from Mr. Ulfson's room and his tablet. Video feeds from that timeframe show no one but him ever entering his room and never show the tablet out of his possession. For instance, he routinely brought it to meals and reviewed documents there. Of course, I could find no indication of a motive for him inserting the virus.

"Second, I analyzed what I could on Mr. Ulfson's tablet, or rather a complete chip-level copy so the original was preserved as evidence. He had fairly sound encryption practice, but I was able to brute force decode a few things and use what little information we had about him to find a bit more. It's very fragmentary, but here's a summary:

- There were quite a few messages that indicate he was in some kind of serious trouble at work. The nature is not clear, but he feared something – exposure, firing, scandal, or some such
- It appears that his trip to Zulea was an attempt to repair this problem, but it didn't go well
- Mr. Ulfson is in a domestic partner relationship with a woman on Tixaya, but several messages suggest this relationship was deeply troubled. He did not appear to be looking forward to returning to his home.
- The data is fragmentary, but the word 'suicide' comes up in various recent files, messages, video, and audio considerably more frequently than a regional norm for references to that term.
- He has a lot of recent activity related to life insurance terms and conditions."

Ximon looked confused. "What are you suggesting? That he killed himself?"

"Captain, I cannot speculate. I am only presenting data that appears to support potential conclusions."

"OK, thanks."

He signaled Iday, "Would you join me on the bridge."

Iday arrived a few minutes later. "Morning, Ximon."

"Good morning. I've got a theory I need to bounce off you. Listen with an open mind and tell me if it's possible."

Ximon laid it out, waving his hands like he was painting an image in the air.

"Let's say that Ulfson is severely depressed, maybe worried about losing his career and his marriage. He's heading home, but there's nothing for him there. He decides to kill himself, but still cares about his life insurance policy paying out for someone or something. So, he does something screwy with the cameras, not to hide a murder from investigators, but to make investigators suspect something. Then, he either tries and fails at several forms of suicide or he intentionally makes it look like murder. He sedates himself with alcohol and sedatives, then he creates bruising around his mouth, gives himself a few shallow stabs in the stomach, and slits his wrists, throwing the knife down the garbage shoot before laying down to die."

"What do you think? Is it possible?"

Iday considered this carefully before answering. "Ximon, that is quite a story. How do we know any of that?"

"We don't, but we know it was he that screwed with the cameras, we're pretty sure he was depressed and interested in life insurance, and we can't see any way that anyone else could have committed the murder. I think he may have 'murdered' himself so he could still get the insurance money."

"How do we prove any of this?"

"I'm not sure that WE can, but perhaps the authorities on Thade can. We'll keep watching for anything else that breaks lose, but otherwise we just keep a sharp eye out so nothing else happens. Then we toss the turd in their lap."

"It sounds far-fetched but it's at least possible. I can't see how anyone else doing it IS possible. The only other theory I could come up with was that either Elsbeth did it (because she could manipulate the camera system so she could sneak in and do it) or that someone else was working with Mantis so they could. That would mean either Elsbeth or you and I don't think either of you has a motive. Even if you did, I think either of you would commit the crime more cleanly so there was less suspicion."

"You forgot two possibilities. It could have been you working with Mantis or Elsbeth to do it. Or, it could have been Raiza, acting on my behalf."

He considered that. "Yes, also theoretically possible. However, I think the crazy suicide idea sounds more plausible."

"Me too. If nothing else I certainly choose to believe that the woman I share my bed with isn't a crazed killer."

Iday nodded sagely. "That is probably prudent. I suspect your sleep would be affected otherwise."

So, the flight continued. Ximon huddled with Mantis and/or the crew repeatedly, but they never found any other way that any other passenger could have done it. At one point they even discussed the possibility that one of the frozen passengers had somehow done it, but the cryo chambers showed continuous, uninterrupted sleep.

The passengers regularly pestered them for answers, but all they could say was, "We continue to investigate and will turn the matter over to the authorities when we reach Thade. We have taken extra security measures to ensure your safety."

Ximon got so sick of the questions that he eventually had Raiza post that answer on the screen in the galley.

The passengers were quite anxious by the time they got out of jump, but there were no incidents. Ximon compiled all of the date they'd uncovered into a consolidated report.

They came out of jump, did their checks, and were safely in the Thade X system, out near the fifth planet with 23 hours to get to the main planet.

As soon as they were safe and enroute, Ximon contacted the system police constabulary and said he had to report that a murder had taken place on his vessel while in jump.

Ximon was given contact information for a Detective Barnato of the Extraplanetary Crimes Division. Ximon messaged him, laid out the general events, sent the report, and asked how Barnato wanted to proceed until they got to the planet.

He got an audio callback from Barnato. "You've given us a lot to chew on here. I'll digest this and will meet the ship when you get here. Just bring the ship and passengers safely here and we'll take it. I can't tell anything until I see the report and we get the evidence, but it looks like you did as thorough an investigation as could possibly be expected."

"Understood. We'll have everything ready for you."

As they headed for the planet Ximon informed the passengers that the local police would want to meet with them briefly upon landing. This irritated them somewhat, especially the lady, but Ximon was past caring. They made it to the planet without incident and landed at a pre-arranged berth.

The crew had pre-planned the debarkation procedure. Raiza accompanied the passengers off where they'd have to wait to talk to the police and get their bags, which Elsbeth and Iday would offload. Ximon would meet with Barnato, hand over physical evidence, show everything of relevance on the ship to him, and hand over the body. Once the luggage was done, Iday would revive and bring down the cryo passengers.

The ship was met by a small knot of police, two in plain clothes and four in uniform.

Ximon went down the ramp and greeted them. One stepped forward, "Captain Sabo, I presume. I'm Detective Barnato. Dr. Grayson and Officer Bralick here," pointing to a woman in plain clothes and a uniformed officer with extra video gear "will accompany us in looking at the ship and retrieve the body. These other officers will have a few questions for the passengers."

"The passengers are all yours. Do with them as you will. Let me show you the areas of interest in the ship."

Barnato signaled something to the other officers and they headed for the passengers.

Ximon took Barnato and team into the ship. First, he showed them Ulfson's room. Bralick took extensive images, Grayson examined the sheets and other bedding, and had Bralick collect them. Bralick also took some readings off the network that Ulfson would have connected to in order to implant the virus. Ximon also briefly showed them the only areas Ulfson was ever detected in – the galley and the showers. They took pictures, but there was little of interest.

Ximon handed over all the physical evidence they had – the knife, Ulfson's tablet and personal effects, and a data cube with all of the relevant security video.

Then he took them to the cryo chamber area. Iday was already there in the process of waking the two cryo chamber passengers. The process took a few minutes, so Iday just stepped out of the way.

Ximon showed them Ulfson's body and again described exactly what tests they'd done before they froze him. At one point, Iday interjected, naming a few medical tests that Ximon overlooked.

When Ximon was done, Barnato looked at his notes and considered. "Captain, we're going to need to take the cryo chamber that Mr. Ulfson's body is in – anything else risks further contamination or damage to evidence."

"No problem, though we'd eventually like it back." Then he nodded to Iday and together they undid the lock-down clamps and lowered the wheels. "It's all yours."

Dr. Grayson said to Barnato, "Ok, we've got this Frank," and she and Bralick wheeled the cryo chamber off.

Barnato then sent Ximon digital receipts for the body, evidence, logs, cryo chamber, etc. and said, "Will you be around for a few days? We may need to ask you and your crew further questions."

"Yes, we'll be in port at least two days."

"... and we might possibly need to come back and do some more analysis on the ship."

"If necessary, just let me know."

By this time, the cryo passengers were up and getting steady. Being frozen for a week or two could be disorienting.

Ximon leaned into Slade as he walked past. "Slade, there was a hot young thing on the ship as a passenger. You'll probably see her once you get down the ramp. She's a HUGE fan of yours." He said with a wink, "You should really say 'Hi.'"

He replied in a gravelly voice, "Yeah, sure man. Thanks. Always good to meet a fan, especially a hot one."

Iday nodded that he would point Thuvia out to him.

Then Ximon escorted Barnato off the ship while Iday finished with the cryo pax.

Barnato shook Ximon's hand, thanked him for his help, and headed off.

Once THAT legal issue was over, Ximon had time to study his messages. He again had a message from the lawyer. They'd had the first judicial hearing, and everything appeared positive. He hoped to hear more within a few weeks.

He told the crew, "Take three days off and meet back here at 0800. We may, or may not, have a job. If we do, I'll let you know if that tweaks our time."

As she went to grab a bag, Elsbeth said, "Well deserved time off, I'd say."

Other than a few follow-up questions from the police, the next few days were restful and uneventful. Ximon spent most of it just strolling around, or lying around, with Raiza. He decided against any involved job as he just wanted to get back to Tixaya without trouble. However, he did agree to haul some physical mail so there was at least a little bit of income.

They took off in three days without incident, got to the jump point, and jumped to Tixaya. Having no one to complicate their lives, the jump there was refreshingly quiet. More relaxation, some study, etc. The only thing of note was that Ximon had Mantis develop a logo for herself and for the crew – a praying mantis emerging from a survey craft. Ximon thought it was pretty cool and the crew liked it. Mantis was also working on an "avatar" of herself to use as video on in meetings and screens. That was going less well and Ximon wasn't sure about the idea. Most of the avatars Mantis had come up with looked a bit like The People they'd met in Avar 4.

And then they were back home to Tixaya, landed, and disembarked.

Ximon announced. "You've all deserved some well-earned rest. Take a week off. I hope to hear something on the salvage soon and I'll let you know."

JAUNT 6: FLYING TO THE FUTURE

Ximon and Raiza were out to dinner a few days later when he heard from the lawyer. They had won the claim! There were, of course, legal fees, dock fees, some legal concessions, etc., but Ximon had been awarded almost 21 million credits!!! In his mind, the Mantis had been awarded that money, but it was really his, though he owed small percentile shares based on Elsbeth and Iday's contracts.

He worked with a local lawyer to ensure he did everything properly as well as generously.

Ximon invited the team all to dinner in a few days at a nice restaurant to discuss. Over the appetizers he gave them the good news. They had won the salvage, though the lawyer and everyone else has taken their pound of flesh. Still, they'd gotten more money than Ximon had ever earned.

"OK crew, we got some good news. We won the salvage and have a tidy sum after all the expenses and vulture's fees. I've put a chunk of that money in an operating account for the Mantis, so we won't need to skimp on parts or operations for a good, long time. I've also bought more shares of the Mantis, so it/we don't owe so long in the ARC. I could have bought almost all of them, but there's not that much of a downside. I also bought a couple shares for each of you, so you're officially five percent owners each and you each have a clause in your contracts that you earn more shares over time of service. Whatever happens, you'll be entitled to a portion of the profits from 'Mantis Missions Inc.' assuming, of course, that we have any. I can't guarantee that."

They raised their glasses at that and then Ximon keyed a

button on his tablet.

"You'll see you've also each received a sizable lump sum payment. That'll cover pay, bonus, etc."

He had given Elsbeth and Iday each close to a million credits, equivalent to six to eight years' pay.

Elsbeth looked twice at her tablet. "Well hell, Ximon. That's not enough to set me up as the Queen of Sheba, but it's definitely a start."

Iday smiled broadly. "That is a most impressive and generous sum. Thank you, Ximon."

"I hope you'll both stay on at a slight raise, but obviously, that's your call. I've also set aside a half million credits for stem to stern repairs of the Mantis. Elsbeth, whatever else you do, I'd like you to coordinate that. If more is needed, take it out of that operating budget."

"Oh, yeah. I'll get her fixed up real pretty and we'll have spare parts and everything!"

Ximon continued, "I assume that'll take about three to four weeks, so I'd hope to take off again in about five weeks. So, other than coordinating those repairs, y'all are on paid vacation."

Elsbeth let out a whoop and raised her glass. "Money, repairs, and vacation!"

Iday echoed, "Hear, hear" and raised his glass.

The next few weeks involved a lot of diverse things, but never enough that they were really busy.

The ship received some significant repairs, upgrades, and TLC from stem to stern. Her hull was patched, washed, and painted including large nose art of their new logo. Her entire fuel system was flushed, and every filter and valve replaced. The jump drive was tuned by a specialist. He insisted they replace a couple coils and a few other components, but the stabilization ratings were far better than they'd ever gotten. The maneuver drives got some upgraded components and professional tuning as well, getting slightly improved output at considerably better efficiency. The comm system was upgraded for better fidelity and range. The sensors were upgraded to much newer models and tuned by an expert, increasing range, data gathered, and analysis capability. The display screens were all replaced, and the crew couches updated. The turret was mounted and "sighted in" by a specialist. A thousand small electrical and plumbing things were fixed. It was pretty much a complete overhaul.

The security system was considerably enhanced, with more and better cameras, increased coverage, and a much better central processing system. They also added a badging system so that all non-passenger areas could only be accessed with a virtual badge on the crew's comm unit and/or implanted chip. Ximon also had a computer security expert come in, completely isolate the passenger/guest network, strengthen overall system security, and ensure that security components would be automatically updated in the future.

Ximon and Raiza oversaw a remodeling of the galley and crew quarters. Everything was stripped down, repaneled or repainted, and new carpet installed. The sink/toilet area was completely redone. They got new countertops, cabinets, appliances and furniture. They also replaced all the beds with new ones that were slightly larger and much more comfortable and got new sheets, pillows, quilts, etc. They also had each room stocked with plush towels, robes, and slippers. The pantry was also completely redone and restocked.

Mantis' computer system was also considerably upgraded. She got enhanced processing power, memory, and storage capacity. All of her software was upgraded to the latest versions and her informational database was almost quadrupled. Her networking was also enhanced so she could more easily interface with any or all tablets or comm units on the ship.

Ximon also got a "telepresence platform" for Mantis, essentially a video screen and cameras mounted on a pole above two wheels. It allowed a more physical form of the Mantis computer to "accompany" them or participate in conversations. The same technology had been used for centuries to represent people who could not be physically present at meetings and such.

Finally, Ximon had ship uniforms designed and made for them. They were nice, comfortable jump suits with a light jacket that could be worn to look nicer. They were charcoal grey and black with the Mantis logo boldly emblazoned on the left chest and their name and position on the right. He had several made for each crew member.

Ximon gave Raiza her uniforms with "Chief Steward" embroidered over the pocket in their stateroom.

She said, "Thank you, Ximon. I appreciate your recognition as part of the crew."

Ximon hugged her. "Raiza, I consider you the crewmember of the year. You're very precious to me."

Raiza kissed him. "As you are to me."

Ximon then did something he'd been thinking about for a while. He took her hand, got down on one knee, and said, "Raiza, will you marry me?" presenting her with a ring; very nice but also safe and sensible for starship wear.

She touched his face affectionately. "Ximon, I could never refuse you anything. Nothing in the universe could make me happier than to be your wife. I will do my best to love you better than I have."

He got up. "You do a pretty dang good job of loving me. We'll arrange the wedding in a few weeks, but why don't you show me that loving part now?" as he pulled her toward the bed.

Mantis wasn't the only one to get an upgrade. Ximon gave Raiza an extended upgrade/spa treatment. He got her a new lower body mobility package known as the Travelling Companion. This basically upgraded her lower skeleton and musculature, so she could better walk extended distances and run. Some of her skin was upgraded – it felt even more real and had more nerves, so she got more sensations of touching things or being touched. Her breasts were slightly enlarged in the process, but that was, of course, just a natural side-effect. She also got enhanced processing power, program upgrades, and a couple new skill routines. In particular, she got a medical skill routine. This provided basic medical knowledge and capability roughly equivalent to a nurse. She came out of the process more beautiful than ever, but also more capable.

Ximon, too, got some "upgrades." He finally had some cosmetic procedures done – what used to be crudely called plastic surgery. Some extra fat around the middle was removed and muscles hydro-electrically toned. His skin received a complete 'sand blasting' (he couldn't remember the proper term) – all moles and tags removed, some wrinkles removed, pores hyper cleaned, and everything moisturized down several levels. His hair was also "thickened," and his teeth whitened.

On a "down" note, Iday asked to meet with Ximon a couple weeks later. He said, "Captain, with considerable regret, I must tender my resignation. I have long desired to serve more fully in my church but have been unable to do so as I would like. I have long saved toward that goal, but your generosity removed the last of my excuses. I have been called to lead a congregation near my hometown. I've also been called to marry a member of that congregation. I haven't met her yet, but she looks attractive in the photo I've been given. I am told that she is lovely, kind, hard-working, and devout. I am confident that she will make me happy and I will endeavor to make her happy."

"Are you sure you two couldn't be happy on the Mantis?

She'd be more than welcome."

"I am afraid that is not how it works. I am sorry that it is not so. I will leave for my congregation in a month."

"Well, I am very, very sorry to see you go. However, as a priest, I would ask one thing of you before you go, if you can."

"Anything I can do, I will."

"I'd like you to marry Raiza and I."

Iday considered that thoughtfully. "Ximon, you know that wouldn't have legal standing in most areas, correct?"

"Yes, and I'm not sure what your god or any other god might think of it."

"Ximon, among other things, a key purpose of marriage is to bind two people together that they may bring one another comfort, joy, and support. I know that you and Raiza cherish one another, so I cannot object, and God would not do so. If you find a location, I will be happy to perform the ceremony. Though I must warn you, it will be my first."

"Thank you, Iday. We'll send you all the details as soon as we can sort them out. When we do, let us know if you need us to adjust anything."

Ximon and Raiza elected to have the ceremony in about three weeks on a small island they could rent most of. Elsbeth and Iday did most of the planning, though they employed a wedding planner of sorts and Raiza and Mantis helped quite a bit.

On the day of the wedding, the island was almost theirs alone with just a few bungalows for guests and a small staff on the other side of the island. Most of the guests were brought to the island the morning of the wedding.

The wedding was on a grassy area just off the beach. The area was subtly, but nicely, decorated and Mantis and the sea served as a nice backdrop.

The "crowd" was not large. A couple of Ximon's siblings were there with their families, including a couple nephews and nieces he liked, as well as his aunt and uncle, and one stray cousin that Ximon had kept in touch with occasionally over the years. He hadn't seen most of them in person for several years, but he was glad they had come.

Raiza had almost as large a group on her side. After Ximon proposed and they set a date, Raiza had visited the offices of TrueForm Service Robots (TSR) where she had been assembled years ago and where all her modifications were made. She had invited the Chief Engineer and quite a few of the technicians or receptionists that she had dealt with. Ximon wasn't sure whether it was the free "destination" wedding or, perhaps, a chance of publicity, but several came, as well as the Regional VP of Development.

Iday officiated, wearing his Mantis uniform and a sash worn by priests of his religion. Ximon wore his dress KSF uniform, which he had had tailored for the occasion. Elsbeth acted as the "best man" and "maid of honor," wearing her Mantis uniform. Mantis attended with her telepresence platform and acted as a witness.

Raiza was walked down the aisle by the TSR Chief Engineer whom she later said was the closest thing to a father she had. She was beyond stunning in a short, stylish lace dress, thin veil, and her now longer hair in ringlets of strawberry gold. Ximon thought that few women could ever have looked so beautiful.

The wedding itself was brief and touching. Ximon and Raiza both wrote their own vows (though Ximon assumed that Raiza had worked with Mantis to search an encyclopedia of all vows in the history of mankind). Ximon's were simple, telling of their strange, but special love. Raiza's were more eloquent and poetic. When Iday pronounced them "man and wife," Ximon lifted the veil and kissed Raiza passionately, happier than he'd ever been.

The wedding was followed immediately by a reception. This lasted quite a bit longer with a nice meal, some toasts (Elsbeth gave the "best man" speech), drinks, gifts, and dancing. It was quite fun. Ximon and Raiza did some dancing (a new skill she had received in her last upgrade and which he had taken a few classes on). Elsbeth drank too much and danced with every man present, including Ximon's uncle and nephews, every man from TSR, and even one of the servers.

They received some nice gifts. Blankets and other bedroom comforts from his family, mementos and wine from Elsbeth, a book of scripture and a scroll on marriage from Iday, and gift cards for free spa days from TSR.

Raiza's first meeting with Ximon's family was a little awkward at first. They were obviously unsure of him marrying a robot. However, Raiza was very charming, thanking them profusely for their gifts and asking them to please let her and Ximon know if they were ever interested in travelling to other planets or systems. She won big points by saying to the teens in a stage whisper, "If you can't get them to go but you want to, let us know and we'll see what we can do." It made her seem human, and every parent appreciates someone showing interest in their children, even if it's a robot. They seemed to warm to her during the reception and Ximon's uncle, cousin, and one nephew danced with the bride.

Ximon and Raiza thanked everyone for their kindness, attendance, and gifts. He especially thanked Iday for conducting and Elsbeth for helping to set things up. He left Iday with the latter saying, "Expect to receive an invitation for my wedding in a few weeks."

Ximon and Raiza headed to their bungalow early and had a fabulous night. The party continued for quite a while before all the guests retired to their bungalows.

The next morning, the crew took everyone to the spaceport nearest their homes and got dropped off themselves. Mantis took herself back to the island on auto-pilot, standing ready for Ximon and Raiza.

Ximon and Raiza had at least half the island to themselves for a week. They spent a lot of time in bed, walking in the hills, or laying on the beach, the latter often nude. Raiza's upgraded skin even had some kind of color crystals in it that responded to sunlight, so she got tan after exposure to a certain amount of sunlight over a period of time and then it faded after days without it. Seeing Raiza with tan lines, and without, was intriguing.

Ximon considered it the most wonderful and relaxing week of his life. He thought of nothing save Raiza and their future together and truly lived in the moment. They talked for hours, primarily with Ximon telling Raiza endless stories about his career and life. In return, she presented ideas of additional things they might enjoy doing together. She had researched this thoroughly with Mantis and had many ideas.

But sadly, all good things must come to an end, and it was eventually time to leave. They left sizable tips for the staff that had been kind, helpful, and (most especially) discrete and took Mantis back to home port.

There they relaxed some more there and generally made the ship ready and settled affairs. One momentous thing they did was buy a small house, so they had somewhere to call home when they weren't flying about. It also gave them somewhere to store the excess gifts or other things they accumulated over time. Among other things, Ximon got a lot of KSF memorabilia accumulated over decades out of storage and put in the house instead.

Ximon and Raiza were relaxing in the now-more-comfortable galley on Mantis when Elsbeth returned. She had a man on her arm who was carrying her bag. As they approached, it became obvious that the "man" was a male companion robot.

Raiza spoke first. "Hello, Elsbeth. I hope you're well."

Ximon waved. "Elsbeth, welcome back. Who's your friend?"

Elsbeth was beaming more broadly than Ximon had ever seen her. "Ximon, Raiza, this is my companion, Peter. He might be the love of my life. He'll be joining me on the ship unless you vehemently object. He will be a big help."

Ximon shook Peter's hand. "Absolutely no objection here. Peter, it's a pleasure to meet you. Welcome to Mantis." He motioned to Raiza. "This is my dear wife, Raiza."

He shook both their hands, Ximon's with a hearty handshake and Raiza's diffidently.

He spoke with a rich, very human voice. "Thank you, captain. Happy to meet you Raiza. It is a pleasure to be here and meet Elsbeth's friends. I will try to be of as much assistance as I can."

Ximon, "I'm sure you will be."

Ximon could barely suppress his laughter, remembering all the ribbing that Elsbeth had given him over the months about Raiza, "So, Elsbeth, how did you two .... meet?"

"Well, Ximon, I've had mixed luck with men. I've seen how happy you and Raiza are, and that got me thinking. Then, at the wedding, I was dancing really close with one of those nice TSR men. He gave me an invitation to tour the factory and gave me a great discount. I took him up on it, looked, and was impressed. I found what I liked, with all the right options, and went for it. I'm having a great time."

"That sounds great. So, Peter, tell us about yourself."

Peter said, "Captain, I am a QT companion/service robot, with a strength enhancement. I have some programmed skill in mechanics and cargo handling."

"Well, then, you will be most helpful."

Elsbeth interrupted excitedly, putting her hand on

Peter's shoulder. "That's not the best part. Peter, take off your shirt."

Peter did so without embarrassment, revealing a heavily muscled chest, big arms, and a washboard stomach. Elsbeth ran her hand down his chest.

She continued, "He's REAL easy to look at. He's hung like a horse, can LITERALLY stay hard ALL night long if I want him to, and he has a tongue like a dog lapping up a river." With this, she winked and nudged Raiza jokingly, "You know what I mean?"

In response, Raiza revealed a new twist to her communication skills saying in a no-nonsense tone, "Oh, you know it, girlfriend!"

Then Raiza looked intently at Ximon and very slowly and sexily rolled her tongue over her lips.

Elsbeth loved that one, bending over laughing.

When she finally caught her breath, she was more serious, waving with her finger in a circle to indicate all of them. "Ximon, we're the wave of the future. Doing this relationship thing with another human, with their own problems, phobias, and hang-ups, is just too hard ... at least for people like us. This is the way to go. Way .... of ... the ... future!"

Ximon both shrugged and nodded. "Well, I'm not sure humanity can survive that." He wrapped his arm around Raiza's waist, "But it's dang sure all I want."

The End